THE PURPLE MANTLE

Emperor Diocletian tortures St. George by tying him to a wheel
(see p. 102).

Fresco from the New Shuamta Monastery in Kakhetia, Georgia.
Copy of an ancient fresco in the Church of St. George at Nakipari in Svanetia,
Georgia, by the royal iconographer Theodore, A.D. 1130. Photograph courtesy
of John Wurdeman, with the blessing of Metropolitan David
of Alaverdi and Telavi.

THE PURPLE MANTLE

(IN THE REIGN OF DIOCLETIAN)

An Historical Novel by Aliki Kafetzopoulou
Translated from the Greek by Efrosyni Zisimou Robinson
Edited by Lawrence Damian Robinson

ST. HERMAN OF ALASKA BROTHERHOOD

2001

Printed with the blessing of His Grace
JOVAN
Bishop of the Serbian Orthodox Diocese
of Western America

Copyright 2001 by
Lawrence Damian and Efrosyni Zisimou Robinson,
and the St. Herman of Alaska Brotherhood

First Printing

Address all correspondence to:
St. Herman of Alaska Brotherhood
P. O. Box 70
Platina, California 96076

Front cover: Great Martyr George before Emperor Diocletian.
Back cover: Great Martyr George.
Fourteenth-century frescos by master iconographer Damiané, located in the Church of St. George in the Ubisi Monastery, Racha, western Georgia.

Library of Congress Cataloging in Publication Data
Kafetzopoulou, Aliki.
    The purple mantle (in the reign of Diocletian).
    Translated from the Greek by Efrosyni Zisimou
    Robinson. Edited by Lawrence Damian Robinson.
Library of Congress Catalogue Number: 2001086925
ISBN 1-887904-05-0

This English translation of *The Purple Mantle* is humbly dedicated to the memory of Rachel Scott of Columbine High School in Littleton, Colorado, and to all the unknown martyrs of our Lord and Savior Jesus Christ, both of the ages past and of those yet to come.

CONTENTS

ACKNOWLEDGMENTS

I wish to give thanks to the following people, without whom this translation would have been impossible.

Firstly, to my dear husband, Damian, for the many and long hours he put into editing this book into its final form, and for always encouraging me to get involved in the translation of Christian books.

To my youngest brother, Augustine, who helped me enormously by providing much needed logistical support in Greece. To my youngest sister, Irene, who spent a good part of her summer "vacation" in America helping me with the translation of this book. To my dearest mother-in-law, Nina, for her love, support and critical review of this translation.

To Abbess Olympiada and Father Mark of the Holy Protection Monastery in Weatherly, Pennsylvania for their constant prayers and support during the translating and editing of this book, and always.

Special thanks to my brothers, Archimandrite Fr. Lucas of Poros and Priest-monk Fr. Nektarios of the Holy Mountain (Athos), and to my spiritual father, Fr. Michael of Bethlehem, Pennsylvania, for their continual prayers.

Also, I would like to thank my beloved parents, Demetrios and Kyriaki Zisimos, who brought me up to love God and His Holy Church, and who first taught me through their own example to put God before everything else.

Finally, this English edition would not be possible without the kind and loving support of Mrs. Aliki Kafetzopoulou, whose beautiful book inspired me so much when I was a young girl growing up in Athens, even as it continues to inspire countless young Christians in Greece today. I only hope and pray that through our humble and wholly inadequate efforts to translate it into English, it may now inspire a generation of young Christians both in America and around the world.

Efrosyni Zisimou Robinson

TRANSLATOR'S INTRODUCTION

As we embark on the dawn of a new millennium, the human race is faced with some of the most challenging issues and questions ever contemplated. From topics such as drug wars, school shootings, Middle East peace and the meaning of national sovereignty on the political and social fronts, to the subjects of global climatic change, cloning and genetic manipulation on the scientific and technological fronts, we are forced every day to think in new ways about how our society will live in the world of the twenty-first century.

And in many ways, it seems that our world is becoming an increasingly atomized, desperate and impersonal one in which the meaning of life and of the individual's relationship with and responsibility to society is ever more tenuous and obscure. Indeed, one often wonders where the world is heading, and whether or not the changes that are occurring at an exponential rate are to be counted as true progress, or merely as the gathering momentum of our social and spiritual decline.

Even among Christians, it often seems in today's hedonistic society that the essential purpose of life in this world—our salvation through the grace of our Lord Jesus Christ and the indwelling of the Holy Spirit, in repentance and love—becomes a compartmentalized and incidental aspect of our daily pursuit of pleasure and financial security.

Yet it is precisely as Christians that we recognize this trend towards technological idolatry and societal fragmentation as a dangerously flawed one. While millions may wonder what lies in store for the human race at the dawning of this great age of technological advancement, we already know what has been laid up for our future. And while we cannot tell whether the things to come will be revealed "like a thief in the night" tomorrow or one hundred or even one thousand years from now, we can be sure of two things. First, in the words of Saint Paul, that "what is obsolete and growing old will soon disappear." And second, that today, in this first year of the second millennium after the birth according to the flesh of our Lord and Saviour Jesus Christ, we are closer to the coming tribulation than at any time in the preceding two thousand years.

It is for this reason that Mrs. Aliki Kafetzopoulou's historical novel, *The Purple Mantle (In the Reign of Diocletian)*, is so important at this time in our Christian history. For not only is it a novel about our past, and about the common heritage shared by all Christians around the world, but it is also a novel about our future. It is a story with one indelible and indispensable message: that for those who love Christ, the passing glory of this world (along with all the material wealth and comfort that may come with it) is worthless. And not only is it worthless, but it can even be a stumbling block and a snare that can keep us from the precious prize of our salvation.

This story brings to life in vivid clarity the choices faced by people very much like ourselves, between the ephemeral comforts and glory of this world and the eternal glory of the world to come. In a certain respect we make these choices daily even now—for example, when we choose television over spiritual reading and prayer, or when we choose the ease of material possessions and the accumulation of wealth over charity and acts of mercy. Yet in a very literal sense, we may someday be forced to make the same choices as many of the characters in the story, at the risk of our very lives. It is our fervent prayer and hope that, as Christians, when the time comes, our choice will be clear. Yet if we do not make the right choices now, when the stakes are immeasurably smaller, can we hope to make the right choices when our very lives are at stake? As our Lord Himself asked, "And yet, when the Son of Man comes, will He find faith on earth?"

Far from having a morbid preoccupation with death, followers of Jesus Christ have a joyful preoccupation with life, the eternal life offered to each one of us by the Lord through His salvific death and resurrection for our sakes. It is thus by remembering and honoring the Christian martyrs—those images of the Lord Jesus Christ, who bear the imprint of His life-giving crucifixion within themselves and who are worthy of Life—that we remember and honor what we are called to be for the sake of the Lord and His Gospel.

In her novel Aliki Kafetzopoulou has skillfully woven a rich historical tapestry full of spiritual depth, in order to present to us a glimpse of the lives of some of the martyred saints of the early Church. And in the process, she also presents us with a subtly told tale of spiritual growth and awakening in the midst of the chaos, confusion and fear of a society run amok in its denial of the True God. Although this is a story that is set in the antiquity of the Roman Empire, it is a story that could easily be told in the context of our twenty-first-century "global empire."

To mention a few technical points: While nearly all of the saints depicted in the story were martyred under the persecutions instituted by the Roman Emperor Diocletian, there are a few whose dates of martyrdom may be debated, and thus it may be that they were actually martyred under earlier or later persecutions, such as those of the Emperors Decius or Galerius. Also, the present translation treats most of the names of the saints and the historical Roman personages mentioned in the story using Greek spelling conventions (for example "Demetrios" rather than "Demetrius"), although either the Greek or Latin conventions are acceptable. The majority of martyred saints mentioned in the story are indicated with an asterisk, and the appendices at the end of the book provide some additional historical and ecclesiastical information about selected martyrs.

Wondrous is our Lord and Savior Jesus Christ in His saints and martyrs! Through their intercessions and shining examples, may the Lord grant us the courage and the faith to overcome the ceaseless persecutions, both spiritual and temporal, waged mercilessly by the enemy of our souls. May the Lord grant us the victory both now and in the age to come.

Damian & Efrosyni Robinson
Eve of the Holy Theophany of Our Lord
and Savior Jesus Christ
January 5, 2000

1

A THOUSAND HOPES, A THOUSAND DREAMS

T HE lively conversation of the group of boys stopped abruptly as the headmaster of the gymnasium suddenly appeared. It was a winter afternoon in the year 303 A.D.

"I think it's time for you to go," he said with his loud and commanding voice, looking at them strictly.

They all stood up from the marble stairs, straightened their tunics and showed that they didn't need to be told a second time. For one thing, they did not want to give the headmaster a reason to complain about them; and for another, they realized that their discussion concerning their impressions and opinions about the day's games had so absorbed them that it was already late and getting dark outside.

The boys left the arcade, which had been built for the Winter Games to protect them from the cold air and the rain, and went out of the gym. The next day would find them there again for their training. The big games that took place in the spring were no longer that far off. Since it was the first time the boys would participate, all their interests and thoughts were focused on the games.

Who would the winner be? they all wondered.

The secret ambitions of each and every one of the boys, nourished for months now from the day's thoughts to the night's dreams, and founded on the praise and inspiration of past victories, were multiplied even further as time went by. But lately, something else had happened.

Today Rufus had dared to say something that every one of them feared, and not one of them thought that his prediction would turn out to be wrong.

As they saw with how much agility and strength Helianos had made that long-jump, leaving behind by fifteen inches their friend Antisthenis, who was always first, the same thought went through all their minds: *Who is going to be the winner of the games?*

Rufus spoke with certainty as they all gathered together by the stairs of the arcade: "We don't need to study philosophy or mathematics to know who!"

"Do you believe it will be Helianos?" one of the other boys asked.

"No doubt about it! He was the last to join the gym, but so far he is first in track and wrestling."

"What about discus-throwing? Don't you remember the other day?"

"Exactly! In discus-throwing, too. And today that jump!"

As much as it went against their secret ambitions, they just could not help but admit that the sixteen-year-old, chestnut-haired boy with the smart expression and the tall, graceful presence would become an obstacle to their success in obtaining the wreath of victory. That was the reason their conversation kept them so late at the gym and continued very vividly on their way back home.

Helianos had left much earlier. With a sparkling look in his eyes and a quick pace, he walked through the streets of the city of Nicomedia full of excited happiness. The redness in his cheeks was neither from the brisk weather nor from the last rays of the setting sun that cast a beautiful red glow around the city. And if an eye could penetrate deep into his heart, it would see that the gym, the long-jump and all the praises there were already forgotten and that other worlds were engaging his thoughts with an unstoppable attraction.

"Hello, Helianos!" a voice coming from out of the marketplace tried to stop him.

It belonged to a certain Adrian,* who had to grab the young man's arm and speak up louder so that he would hear him, so lost was Helianos in his thoughts.

"Could you help me move somebody to the doctor?" he asked him quickly.

"Now? Impossible!… They're waiting for me," Helianos answered, showing that he did not want to add anything else.

He did not intend to change his route for anyone. Of course Pantoleon,* that young doctor with the handsome face and even more beautiful soul, who was so famous in Nicomedia, was only a couple of blocks away; still Helianos did not have the time, nor was he in the mood to do charitable works. He repeated to Adrian, his wealthy neighbor, that he was in a hurry, and continued at a faster pace and with a brighter redness in his cheeks. This night was going to be so important for him!

The shops had started to light the large oil lamps outside of their thresholds. The shop-owners would also usually put

---

* Asterisks denote actual historic personages who were martyred for their faith in Christ. A list of selected martyrs mentioned in this story, along with the dates of their commemoration by the Orthodox Church, appears in Appendix I at the end of this book.—Ed.

small olive-oil lamps on top of their long wooden tables so that they could see while they collected and counted their money, which was always quite a lot.

Ever since the Emperor Diocletian had come to reside in Nicomedia, making it the capital of the eastern Roman Empire,[1] the city had taken on a more brilliant appearance. Palaces of unimaginable luxury had been built, and the mansions of the senators and the military commanders decorated the new streets and the parks in the center of the city's quarters. Beautifully landscaped gardens with colorful flowers and trees surrounded the mansions of the well-to-do, and the sea of the nearby Astakenos Gulf both refreshed the city and brought ships with goods from all the ports from around the world.

For this reason the shops made large amounts of money every day from their numerous customers. The merchant Urvinos earned even more than the average, because he provided textiles to all the senators and very often to the palace of the Emperor himself. He would import gold-embroidered textiles from Alexandria and Babylon, beautiful purples from Tyre, and fine silks from the island of Kos.

Urvinos had a special tailor who would prepare the colorful attire of the wealthy magnates as well as the distin-

1. Upon coming to power in A.D. 285, Emperor Diocletian reorganized the Roman Empire, dividing it into two administrative regions and appointing a co-Emperor, Maximian. The eastern Roman Empire (the foundation of the powerful Byzantine Empire which lasted until A.D. 1453) stretched from the shores of the Adriatic Sea across Greece and Asia Minor to Persia, and southward through the Middle East to the Holy Land and northern Africa. Its seat of power for much of Diocletian's reign (A.D. 285 to 305) was the city of Nicomedia, known today as Izmit, in modern Turkey.—ED.

guishing robes of the military commandants: white with a thick red chevron around the edges for the Praetorian Guard and the consuls; and dark purple robes, adorned with gold and decorative branches of palm-trees, for victorious generals to wear at public celebrations.

Helianos rushed into the store of his father, Urvinos, so impetuously that he knocked over the oil lamp that a slave was trying to hang by the door. The thick wick of the lamp went out, splattering drops of oil everywhere and causing dark stains to appear on some of the textiles lying nearby, as witnesses to this sudden damage.

Urvinos, beside himself with anger, violently fell on the slave and began beating him pitilessly, while Helianos hurriedly moved to the back of the store, indifferent to the view of what was happening, as if the incident had nothing to do with him.

He rushed upstairs to the workshop of the tailor and highhandedly demanded his new cloak from him. The tailor's reply, that a small finishing touch was needed, made Helianos angry and he began to threaten the old man. Once again, everyone in the store thought how much the son was like his father, harsh and tyrannical.

The small finishing stitch did not take long to complete, and Helianos, taking the mantle and putting it on, looked at himself with pride in the framed brass mirror. He then whispered a few words to his father and left for the mansion of the great General, Teaos. How long did he stay there? Exactly what words did they exchange? How many flutters of excitement did his young heart feel? He could not even begin to describe his feelings.

A thousand hopes, a thousand dreams were rocking him back and forth; other worlds were calling to him with an irresistible allure. There, in those other worlds, were anchored all his hopes and personal ambitions, which were by no means any higher than the hopes and ambitions preoccupying all his friends at the gym.

It was only once he got home that the crystalline laughter of little Ione—who came to greet him, running with her bare feet along the marble tiles of the long entrance hall—made him feel like a kid again. He picked up his little sister in his arms and started singing to her while carrying her into the living room, where a fire was burning in the magnificent marble fireplace. Ione was a little creature, just two years old, sweet and tender with blue eyes and curly black hair, and she always gave him something of her carefree charm.

"Welcome!" said Pavla, his other sister, on seeing him come in. "Rhodon was looking for you at noon, but I didn't know where you were!"

The big brother laughed.

"And you won't find out for the time being, either. Maybe later."

Pavla received his reply with displeasure. She leaned on the delicate shawl that she was embroidering with a colorful rhomboid pattern. The reflection from the fire not only illumined her fine features but also showed her expression of anger caused by the rebuff.

"Dinner is ready!" Kyrianna the servant announced, pulling to one side the curtain that separated the living room from the dining room.

Two lamps placed high above shone and poured out their light around the dining room. The delicious smell from the roasted hen, the freshly baked little loaves of bread and the various salads and appetizers, showed that in Urvinos' home everything was always lavish. And everything was taken care of by the hands of the mistress of the house herself, Helianos' mother, Tatiani.

She was the last to enter the dining room, tall, fine, full of charm and affection. Her pale, pretty face contrasted sharply with her curly hair of darkest ebony. She would always smile as she hugged her children, all of whom bore close resemblance to her. She would take her seat at the table and happily serve everyone herself.

Tonight, however, Tatiani was almost unrecognizable. The dark circles around her eyes emphasized her paleness, and her gaze seemed cloudy. She seemed not to be looking anywhere.

Is Mom ill? Helianos worried to himself.

As rough as they said he was, he loved his mother deeply. But whatever the matter was, the news he had to tell her in a little while would be enough to take away every sadness, he thought, trying to push away his worry.

The evening went by with the usual announcements of the children's daily activities, and with Grandpa's narration of stories about his homeland in Thessalonica. Grandpa's long separation from there filled him with nostalgic memories, and he never missed a chance to revive that beautiful city in front of everyone's eyes with his vivid descriptions. He would talk about Alexander the Great and his exploits, and about his beloved Macedonian land and his desire to see it again. And he would always end by saying, "A trip up there, Urvinos! We should think about it!"

The father usually didn't reply, but Helianos and his brother, Antiochos, would always agree enthusiastically.

At this moment, though, Helianos had other dreams and plans, and he did not seem to be part of the conversation. Of course, along with this fantastic turn of events that was happening to him, he would have to accept some losses as well.

Distractedly eating his favorite pie made with apples and walnuts, he brought to mind his victories that afternoon at the gym. His loss would be that he would miss the big games that would offer him a chance for great glory. It would have been an important advantage for his future development, for his peers and his seniors to know that, at the age of sixteen, Helianos Cronion, son of Urvinos, had received the winning wreath in running; that Helianos Cronion had received the winning wreath in discus-throwing; that Helianos Cronion had come in first in the long-jump; in other words, that Helianos Cronion, son of Urvinos, was exceptional in his abilities and was worthy of every honor!

He did not doubt, of course, that he would find another chance to show off his abilities. But he still did not stop wanting this glory in the stadium, in the presence of all the people of Nicomedia. But what could he do? When all those games were to be happening, he would be so far away!

Dressed in his new uniform, given new responsibilities, he would let his gaze wander on the blue waves, on to the crowded cities, to distant shores. And upon arriving in the famous Alexandria, he would give himself over wholly and with zeal to the responsibilities of his new position, without anyone having to remind him of them.

And he would let his heart overflow with pride and boasting as he walked through the streets of Alexandria, that great city that had been built by Greek-Macedonians, he being a Greek-Macedonian himself!

Countless times as a child he would unroll the old cylindrical scroll from Grandpa's library, in which one could read all about the city of Alexander the Great. It was that city that had transferred the light of ancient Greece to the furthest reaches of Africa, the Macedonian Greek spirit and culture to the land of the Nile!

Sitting at the edge of the chair in his room, with the scroll unfurled on his knees, he would imagine the beautiful marble buildings and the palaces of the Ptolemies[1] with their exotic gardens.

In his thoughts he would face the port of Alexandria and the famous towering lighthouse, which would shine far out across the sea. Or he would wander around the huge halls and rooms of the world's most famous museum, where all the sciences and arts were taught in Greek by the greatest philosophers. One moment he would imagine opening his arms and grabbing hold of one of the volumes out of the six hundred thousand that were packed neatly on the shelves, and the next he would observe with interest the workshops where the leaves of papyrus were prepared to be turned into copies of the already-existing books. He already knew that, with the passing of the centuries, many things had changed. But still, nothing would stand in the way of the pride that would soon fill him as he would through the streets of Alexandria.

While Helianos was absorbed in his thoughts and his sister Pavla was finishing the embroidered shawl that she would

1. The *Ptolemies* were the dynasty founded by the Greek general, Ptolemy Soter, who ruled Egypt and its territories after the death of Alexander the Great in 323 B.C., until their defeat by the Romans about 30 B.C. One of its best-known rulers was the famed Queen Cleopatra.—Ed.

wear tomorrow at the celebration of the Terminalians,[1] the conversation was limited to only Grandpa and Antiochos.

Tatiani embraced the bent heads of those around the table with her look, and the dark circles around her eyes seemed even bigger. No one paid attention to her this time. They all had things to do, and it was time for them to go.

---

1. The celebration of the *Terminalians* was an annual Roman festival held in honor of Terminus, the god of boundaries and borders.—ED.

2

"I, GAIOS AVRILIOS DIOCLETIAN, HEREBY DECREE ..."

H OLDING the golden tray with the precious cup made of crystal and fine silver, Mertios moved forward with slow steps, his head bent. The warm milk that the Emperor had asked for was ready for him, but as the guard opened the curtain and the servant entered the room, he did not hear the Emperor giving him permission to proceed. Hesitantly he glanced up. No one was in the room.

The armchair carved of ebony wood was thrust away from the front of the imperial desk, showing that the August One[1] had just left.

Mertios stood there irresolutely. Should he stand there or should he leave the tray and go? He approached the desk with fear. Its four edges were covered with ivory and sapphires, and they shone beautifully as the golden candelabra with its detailed craftsmanship cast a rich light through the precious stones.

Tall marble columns with gold-plated capitals, and walls with colorful frescoes and semiprecious stones surrounded the imperial office. Upon the ceiling were fine reliefs, unique

1. From the time of the first Roman Emperor, Octavian, the Emperor was known by the title of "Augustus," or the August (Noble) One.—ED.

in both their quantity and their variety of gold and stained glass. The most expensive Persian carpets covered the exquisite mosaics. Large pipes for hot air were under all the floors of the palace, and one could certainly say that, for Diocletian's palace, the cold winter of Nicomedia did not exist.

The palace had been built by the best architects of the Empire. Not only did it compete with the fairy-tale palaces of the Orient in luxury and wealth, but with its various apartments it could offer its residents the best stay for every season.

Diocletian believed that by showing off his wealth, he would keep the prestige of the Emperor before his subjects and the other nations. He took into serious consideration how to dazzle them with his grandeur. Instead of the military uniform that all emperors used to wear at that time, he would dress up in a silken, gold-embroidered mantle. The gold bay-leaf wreath that emperors used to wear he replaced with a diadem decorated with the most expensive and unique mother-of-pearl. Even his sandals shone with emeralds and rubies under his valuable purple mantle.

Who would dare to object to or resist a master like him, who was unique on earth for his pomp and power? Who would find the courage to raise his voice or to lift up his head to him, since even the official delegates of foreign states and the great functionaries of the Empire had to salute him by kneeling in front of him and kissing the edge of his gown with great respect? Who would ever think of rebelling against him or against his will and his orders?

Mertios finally decided to leave the tray on his desk. As he put it down, he noticed that a long written parchment with the seal of the Emperor was wide open in front of his eyes. He thought that it probably contained one of the orders of his master, which even went so far as to set the prices of different goods in the market.

Mertios, having been a Christian since he was twelve years old, had never allowed himself to look with curiosity on things that were not his business. And even more so did he behave with respect toward the documents of the Emperor, even though he, as a manservant, would often need to either keep them in his custody or transfer them to someone else. This time was no exception. He did the same as always. He left the tray with the hot drink covered next to the parchment and turned to go, when suddenly he heard the hoarse voice of Diocletian from behind a thick velvet curtain.

"Tomorrow the order is going to be announced! I, Gaios Avrilios Valerios Diocletian, hereby decree:

—All the temples of the Christians are to be demolished!

—All their religious books are to be destroyed!

—Any Christian who holds a high office in my Empire is to be removed!

—All Christians freed from slavery are once again to become slaves!"

Oh my God! Mertios thought to himself in horror. "My God!... Persecution!" he whispered through tightened lips.

Up until now, Diocletian had never persecuted the Christians. Rather, he had ignored them. He had put up with them. He did not even get upset when, staring from the huge verandas of the palace, he saw the roof of the main temple of the Christians standing out, imposing itself among the other buildings in Nicomedia.

Why now?…

How easy it is for the human heart to change suddenly! It is so easy for it to become insensitive, tough and inhuman, when it becomes clouded by the flawed logic of egotism, and when it pays attention to the cunning words of some evil person.

Galerius, whom Diocletian had appointed as Caesar[1] of the Illyrian provinces, and who was also his son-in-law, was a fanatical enemy of the Christian faith; and that was precisely the role that he played. That horrible order would probably never have existed if Galerius had not incited and instigated it.

Mertios put his hand to his clammy, sweaty forehead. Quick as lightning, his thoughts brought to mind their beloved Bishop Anthimos* and their crowded Church in their fair city, which was blossoming not only in the number of the faithful but also in their high level of virtue and Christian steadfastness. He summoned into his mind images of all the brothers and sisters.

But even so, for the officials to lose their high offices, or for the freed slaves to lose their freedom, or even for their churches to be demolished did not seem so terrible to him. Because even without high offices and bodily freedom, he thought, the soul can still live happily. As for the churches, they would build new ones. They would dig down into the ground and build catacombs. They would find a thousand ways to gather together for the worship of their Lord.

But if they lost their books?

---

1. *Caesar* was the title given to the co-Emperors' appointed deputies and successors, who had broad administrative powers over provinces within the Roman Empire.—ED.

Oh, that seemed to the young servant to be the most cruel rule of this persecution! If the scrolls and the parchments with the selections from the Gospels, the Epistles, the Psalms and the other holy writings were destroyed, how could they replace them? Where would they again find the Law of God that delights the heart and refreshes the soul, that encourages the will and teaches virtue? God's Law that comforts in affliction and distress, that allows one to endure hardships, that inspires one in the spiritual race and keeps the Christian a Christian ...

His eyes were full of tears caused from the pain of this threat. He thought of grabbing the order and tearing it apart into a million pieces. But that would only make the persecution worse. The only thing that he could really do now was to run like the wind and inform them.

A large group of young Christians had been gathering for the past two months at Adrian's* countryside villa, and they were copying holy books for the new faithful who had been baptized by Bishop Anthimos. Three hundred and fifty books, Mertios had heard, were finished and were already at Adrian's house in Nicomedia. What a triumph it would be for Diocletian's soldiers if this treasure fell into their hands! Mertios had to act fast and do everything he could to save them. He also had to inform all the brethren about the order before it became public, so they would have time to hide their own books.

Mertios would ignore any danger to his own personal well-being, in order to protect this priceless food for the soul from the approaching catastrophe. He tiptoed out of the room, reached the door and left in a hurry. The guard had already been whipped by his officer that day because he had been late, and so he was not in the mood to joke around as he usually was. The doorman who was responsible for the gateway of the servants, seeing the manservant of the Emperor running along in such a hurry, thought that he must have had an order from him, and so he let him go out quickly without asking him any questions.

Mertios first went to see Father Nikandros and then he went towards the eastern quarter of the city, which was almost entirely Christian. Along the way he met a precious ally, Rhodon, who was coming back at a lively pace from the house of Helianos, without having found him at home.

"Rhodon, difficult days are coming...."

"Why? Do you know something, Mertios?"

"If I'm not wrong about this, I heard that tomorrow the order will be announced."

"What order?"

"Against us!"

"What are you talking about, man? Persecution?"

"Yes, but in a different form. They will demolish our churches and destroy our books!"

"Oh! Soon we'll hear other threats, too. Wish for me to be 'faithful until the end,' Mertios!"

"We should wish the same thing for one another."

"What can we do now? We have to inform all our brothers to hide their books...."

"We've already started that. Do you think your mother will allow you to take the horse to Adrian's house in the country?"

"Yes, I know. It's necessary to go there. She will let me. We should try to save the books they copied out two days ago."

In a very short time Rhodon was riding his horse and, with his mother's blessing, was leaving Nicomedia headed for the countryside, while Mertios was knocking on the door to Adrian's house in the city.

Right next door to the beautiful, newly built mansion of Urvinos stood the comely, old, noble house of Adrian, which he had inherited from his father. Maintaining the old house well without needless extravagance and luxury, they used it for hospitality and for every need of the work of the Church. Adrian and his young wife, Natalia,* were constantly willing to offer not only their home and their money but also much of their personal time for these great necessities.

When Mertios arrived at their home, he found Natalia wrapping the papyrus documents and tying them up in the middle with a thin red ribbon. Adrian, who had to carry a man bedridden with illness to Pantoleon, the doctor, was waiting for their turn to be seen and would be delayed there. The message that Mertios gave to Natalia upset her.

"They will probably search the houses. They might even ask us to turn them over ourselves," said the servant, lowering his sad eyes.

"I'll give my life, but I'll never give up our books!" said Natalia with quiet inner strength.

She looked at the pile of parchments and papyrus scrolls with love.

"As long as Adrian and I live, nobody will touch these books," she added.

"Yes, but maybe we won't be living much longer. The books should be protected to support the generations that come after us," Mertios insisted. "Father Nikandros said that everything should be transferred immediately from your house to another place, to be hidden where nobody would think of searching."

"Then it's going to be as he said," she agreed humbly, and sent a servant to look for Adrian.

3

THE TREASURES
ARE IN DANGER

A soft knock on the narrow little window with the stained glass made Tatiani rise from her seat. She took Ione, who was playing with a thick tassel from her sewing basket, and brought her to be watched by the maid, Kyrianna. Then, turning back to her small workshop, she closed the door and the heavy curtain that concealed it from the rest of the house and went toward the little window.

The soft voice of Natalia, softer than ever, from the other side of the window made her realize that this communication was about something very serious. When Urvinos was building the house, he had put this little window at the corner of her workshop more as a decorative element than as a source of light, since it looked directly at the walls of the neighboring house. But a sisterly love wasted no time in seizing the opportunity to open the adjacent window of Natalia's mansion next door. This secret window, overlooking their gardens and unseen from the street, now served as an element of hope and a source of encouragement to help the newly faithful Tatiani with her difficult struggle as a Christian in her own pagan house.

Two weeks before, Tatiani had been baptized secretly in a small church outside of the city. Except for a few clergymen and the family of Adrian and his wife, Natalia, no one else knew anything about her new life. That was because of her husband, Urvinos. For Tatiani knew that if he ever found out about it, he would explode with tremendous anger at her decision. For this reason her baptism was kept a secret from many, including her own children.

Natalia would often pass papyrus scrolls with writings from the Holy Bible through the little window, or she would repeat to the new Christian the sermon they had heard at church that day.

"What is my little window of joy offering me today?" Tatiani used to say to herself, every time she heard the familiar tap at the window. She would smile with happiness at Natalia and there, in the half-dark slit of that wall, she found the beauty that no other room in her house—however sunlit—could offer her.

That evening Natalia did not want to give Tatiani anything. Instead she actually wanted to ask her something. Along with telling her the disturbing news about the approaching persecution of the Christians, she asked for her opinion and her help in solving her dilemma.

"We are hiding many holy books in the house, and now they are in danger," Natalia said with deep sadness. "Even more so because we are well known as Christians, like many of the other brothers and sisters in Nicomedia. We have to move all of them to a safe place where no one will be suspicious. So I thought, Tatiani, about your father's land in the countryside. The land is so big and uncultivated that no one …"

"Oh! Father's land …," Tatiani sighed.

She knew very well what Christian books were about. She also knew with how much love the faithful studied them, and with how much awe and reverence they kept them. She knew with how much fervent desire and thirst for spiritual knowledge they would painstakingly copy them out and share them with each other, like precious objects or relics. And now to lose them?

"Father's land! Urvinos sold it!" she said sadly, thinking that she would not be able to help. "Even if we still had the land, it would be very dangerous to pass everything through the market, near the military officers' quarters...."

"Dear God, please help us to resolve this matter!" Natalia whispered, knowing that all the other options she had discussed with Adrian and the rest of the brethren had many disadvantages.

Tatiani stared at her with a compassionate look. A few moments ... How many things could happen in a just few moments? As many as there were stars in the sky, and as great as eternity, either for good or for evil!

She was not really looking or paying attention, but her mind was talking—her heart, the heart of a mother, was talking. She thought about Ione, her pretty little angel, stretching out her little arms and stammering her first words of complaint, looking at her with her little blue eyes full of tears.... Then she thought about Antiochos, her thin, sickly Antiochos, and also about her beloved daughter, Pavla, down on their knees, crying and begging her.

And then Helianos ... her tough, proud eldest son with his many talents and his impetuous character. It seemed to her that he looked at her with love and then with pain, anger and hatred, the same as his father. She imagined that they would both decide to betray her....

Oh, a mother's heart! She felt a thousand knives piercing

her heart, trying to stop her, warning her not to make the daring decision, speaking to her with a thousand echoes and voices against the harm that she was planning to do to herself and her family.

A thousand voices in a few moments!

And suddenly they paused, and the piercing knives went back into their sheaths, and the heart of the mother turned back into the heart of a Christian. Oh, that heart of the Christian!

Intrepid and resolute, she stood up with a kind of strength different from any that she had ever known before. She felt that she could confront thousands of enemies.

"Who can separate us from Christ's love?" … "*Whoever loves son or daughter more than Me, is not worthy of Me….*"

The words of God, the few that she knew, came to her aid to strengthen her in making this very great, heroic decision. Her pale face suddenly took on a rose color. Her eyes shone.

"There is a solution, Natalia!" she said animatedly.

"Tell me, what do you think?"

"Yes! I'm thinking …," she said, taking a deep breath and continuing with strength: "Give them here to me, Natalia. No one would ever suspect Urvinos' house! I'll hide them here in my workshop where only the little children come in. I believe God will help to keep them intact and secure!"

"But what are you going to do with them if you are in danger, Tatiani?" asked Natalia with tears in her eyes.

"If it comes to that, then it means that God's call will have come for me, and He will give me the courage to endure anything! Please pray for me!"

Later, hand to hand through the two little windows, all the papyrus documents with the holy writings were transferred from the Christian house of Adrian to the pagan house of Urvinos, without anyone noticing.

In the rosewood trunk in her workshop, Tatiani kept all her textiles and the fabrics for the children's clothes and for the needs of her household. No one ever touched her things, and Urvinos never entered her private little room. She was calm, peaceful and felt sure that the books would not be in danger with her.

She carefully wrapped the scrolls with textiles, put them at the bottom of the rosewood trunk, and covered them with some linens and silk. Then, putting some wool rags on top, she locked both of the trunk's locks securely.

Natalia was watching, praying from her heart. When they bade each other good night, they wished to each other God's strength for the difficult days that were waiting for them.

"Pray for my Helianos," said the mother, worried. "I'm so afraid for him, growing up in our times."

Was it the maternal uneasiness about the dangers faced by her son that painted those dark circles around her eyes, or was it her own anxiety and anguish over the newly initiated persecution of the Church? Who could really read her inner thoughts? And who could actually confirm that it was not the former, since she knew Helianos' dreams and ambitions?

That was why, that evening at dinner, Tatiani had seemed so different than ever before. And her heart tightened even more when, after dinner, Helianos took her in private and enthusiastically announced his plans to her. Was it the praise of General Teaos that had influenced her son? Was it Helianos' own self-confidence and his vanity concerning his handsome presence and his abilities that had pushed him to get involved in such dreams about his future?

Of course, his father's weakness for his eldest son, the constant flattering from his fellow students who wanted his friendship, and he himself, who did not know how to struggle for something higher and more spiritual, could not be held blameless.

When, already late in her life, Tatiani had discovered the only Truth, she had tried to advise her son in her own way. But it was already too late to change his way of thinking and his dangerous ambitions. And now those ambitions were reinforced even more as a result of the General's efforts.

General Teaos was a close relative of the Empress Alexandra, so he could easily surmount the barrier of the strict imperial etiquette that applied to anyone who wanted to enter the palace. And what was more, he was even allowed to see the "divine" face of the Emperor, which was unseen by the people most of the time, except perhaps during a few grand celebrations.

Teaos, who was an old friend of Urvinos (and whom the latter provided with expensive textiles and furs "for free," in exchange for the military protection of his trading caravans), had been glad to meet the merchant's son Helianos, as athletic and handsome as he was.

"He is exactly what the August One needs for his corps of attachés," he had said to Urvinos. "Just write him off from trading rags, Urvinos, and let me promote him. You won't regret it!"

And now their first hopes were beginning to materialize, and those first seeds they had cultivated so carefully were already starting to bear fruit.

Teaos' evening summons to Helianos was so that he could

announce this momentous news to the boy: the General had been informed that he would be allowed to take the son of Urvinos with him as an official attaché on his upcoming mission to tour some regions of the Empire. In this way, the boy was expected to become experienced in military life, so that later he would be prepared to enter the Imperial Guard.

"Your career could be brilliant!" added the General with evident satisfaction, at the same time hiding the subtle reference underlying his words.

But, for Helianos, this hint was no secret. In fact, many people, even the simplest people of the Empire, would understand what the General alluded to. Who had Diocletian once been? Nothing more than the son of a Senator's slave! He had joined the army at a very young age, he had advanced through the ranks to higher positions during the reigns of Emperors Avrilianos and Provos, and then after a little while he himself had been declared Emperor! It was therefore very well known that anyone who was capable, who could assert himself with his charisma and ability, and who could exert his own influence on the Emperor and the army, would have the possibility of someday becoming the Emperor.

Besides, there was much talk about several excellent and brave men who, even now, were close to Diocletian and who could eventually succeed him and govern the vast empire splendidly. First of all there was the Chiliarchos[1] Constantine,* the son of Caesar Chloros, whom Diocletian was holding hostage close to himself in order to guarantee his father's

---

1. *Chiliarchos* (from the Greek word for "leader of a thousand") was the official title of a military commander of high rank (just as *Centurion*, from the Latin word for a hundred, was a leader of one hundred men).—ED.

fidelity.[1] Then there was Count George,* the famous officer of the Imperial Guard, who, because of his excellent presence, his courage and heroism, and especially his brilliant and firm character, left everyone speechless who met him or saw him for the first time.

"George is not that far from the Purple Mantle,"[2] Teaos, who especially admired the Count, had once told Helianos.

"Oh, yes!" the boy agreed.

"So Helianos? What do you think? Isn't it worth it to follow in his footsteps?"

Helianos blushed and did not speak. He did not want to admit that this was also his ambition: that he was dreaming of someday having the Purple Mantle around his own shoulders.

But tonight, in talking to his mother after dinner, Helianos did not hide from her his dreams. He tried a thousand different ways to make her happy and excited about this trip with General Teaos, and about his recognition and placement by the Emperor.

But she stayed silent.

1. In ancient times it was common for rulers to keep the close family members of their rivals and enemies as hostages, as a way to ensure their political and military submission.—ED.

2. In many ancient cultures, purple was considered a royal color (in part because of the expense of obtaining the natural dyes that were produced by crushing certain types of shellfish, or by extracting them from other exotic sources). The Purple Mantle (or Robe) was therefore a coveted symbol of great power and royalty worn only by kings and emperors. Compare this with the crude purple robe that the Roman soldiers thrust onto Christ before his crucifixion, in order to mock him as "King of the Jews."—ED.

"So you mean that I shouldn't have any ambitions?" the young man complained intensely.

"Ambitions are not forbidden, Helianos," she replied. "The desire for glory is implanted within us to inspire us to hope for a better future. The desire for something greater ..."

"Then why aren't you happy for me, Mom?"

"I'm glad, and I'll be even more happy when I hear that you are thinking not only out of ambition and pride but also seriously. And you would think twice about what you are about to do, if only, along with the glory that the Purple Mantle offers, you desired the glory that virtue gives, that kindness ..."

"Oh! I don't understand a thing you're saying!" he answered back, upset. "When somebody becomes great, he can do everything perfectly!"

"Not at all, Helianos! Somebody who becomes great can also commit the greatest crimes. I want you to remember this!"

Tatiani's mind went straight to the decree of the persecution of the Christians, and to the many other decrees, written and signed by the hands of the wearers of that Purple Mantle, that had watered the Tree of the Church with many streams of the blood of the martyrs. She shivered....

Due to his innocence and youthful inexperience, her son was intentionally falling under their influence. What would the future bring? Maybe the sword of the executioner against her, guided by his very own hand!

"Holy God save him!" she whispered as he was leaving.

The dark circles around her eyes grew larger.

Soon, when all the oil lamps in the house were put out,

the newly built little palace of Urvinos, with its spacious halls and rooms and its glass-enclosed circular veranda overlooking the distant sea, wrapped the dreams, or the wakefulness, of its inhabitants in an impenetrable veil of darkness.

It was early in the morning, as the dawn was breaking, when a red glow slowly appeared towards the western side of the city. It went out, and then suddenly a huge fire blasted the sky of Nicomedia.

Helianos, who had already been awake for some time, jumped up with curiosity and went towards the window.

"Fire!" he whispered, full of worry. "What could be burning?"

The wind blew harder and, along with the red shine, brought to his ears the muffled sounds and echoes of a disturbance. He heard the footsteps of a man running, then others and others still.

From the neighboring houses they opened their windows and exchanged conversations.

"What is it? What is happening?"

A slave, carrying a huge basket on his back, seemed to be coming from that direction.

"What's happening?" he said. "I can't even describe it to you! They set a fire in the biggest church of the Christians! It was full of people, thousands[1] of them!"

"Thousands?!"

"And they were burned!"

"Why did they burn them? Who did this?"

---

1. Twenty thousand* Christians were martyred in the blaze.—ED.

"The Second-in-Command and the Emperor's soldiers! Some of them said they had been ordered to burn only the Christian icons and then to demolish the church, but now the fire is going out of control through the roof and the people are being burned alive inside like human torches. Nobody knows how this evil started!"

"Evil? Come on! It's not that evil if it's going to cleanse the place from dirty creatures like them—those unfaithful, unlawful, impious things!" they heard an angry voice saying. It belonged to a trader, who was passing by with dried fruits on his way to the market early in the morning so as to find a good spot and thereby secure enough clientele.

The neighbors, some of whom could not believe the news that the slave had brought them, and some of whom could not even comprehend the events, started talking loudly and making dramatic hand gestures. Some others who were more curious were already in the street going to the place to see for themselves what was going on, and still others brought to mind with agony some of their own relatives and friends who might be there.

Helianos stood there for a while thoughtfully, without seeing or hearing anything around him. In his mind's eye a shiny, refreshingly happy face suddenly appeared in flames before him.

"Rhodon!"

Oh gods! Was Rhodon with them? Neither Helianos' amicable advice nor his scathing ironies had done anything to change his friend's mind. Rhodon remained a Christian, and behaved like a Christian in their school and at the gym, without being influenced by his words and without thinking that their childhood friendship could be threatened.

In the past month, since he had changed schools and enrolled in Babylas' Academy, he had become more steadfast and fearless. Now he was probably with the rest of them in that church.

In the fiery illumination, Helianos thought for a second that he was facing the shiny, dark face of Rhodon, looking at him with his warm brown eyes and whispering to him with an expression of happiness, exactly as he had once told him: "If you only knew.... If you only wanted to know, Helianos, what my faith means! Even dying for it is sweet...."

But Helianos, on the contrary, had stated that he didn't know, that he did not want to know, nor would he ever want to learn about it, and they had cut off the conversation there. Rhodon had remained uncorrected. Whose fault was it?

Helianos shook his head to drive away the uninvited image of Rhodon wrapped in flames that closed his eyes and shut his lips, leaving behind only traces of happiness. He looked once more toward the fire, called to mind the conversation with General Teaos the night before and, turning to go into his room, he shouted with obstinacy, "Everything the August One is doing is right!"

4

A STEEP DECLINE

Ursus timorously raised his head over the gate of the wooden fence and looked around carefully. Every move, every footstep, darkened his glance, made his breath hot and made him push his head back behind the fence with the half-dried bushes.

In these last days there was deep, inconsolable mourning in Nicomedia. How many had died? How many thousands of Christians had found a martyr's end that early morning in the flame-engulfed church? No one was able to tell. No one could count the number of those who had been away from the city and their homes—homes that were now being locked down and pillaged by Diocletian's soldiers, while most of their owners had either left this earth wearing the wreath of martyrdom or were fleeing to the surrounding mountains and deserts.

But Ursus wouldn't go!

How could he go through such horrible things in this brisk winter cold? Thanks to his friend who had given him this tiny, out-of-the-way hut, nobody who knew him could ever trace him. And if that Mertios had not happened to see him that night playing at dice, he would not have been afraid that anyone would suspect he had changed. Nobody!

But he had seen him. Mertios was surprised, and with

brotherly love he had suggested that it was not proper for him to be in that group. He had made his suggestion with pain and sadness. Ursus had seen it. But he had just become upset and told him that he was of age and knew how to protect himself without advice and remarks.

Of course his new friends would give him advice also, but theirs was easy to follow. They didn't ask him to sacrifice and to fight against his passions like the Christians did. His new friends told him always to look to his own advantage and well-being—especially about his own personal safety. They did not ask him to make personal sacrifices.

To have to make personal sacrifices is an ugly thing for a … for a person, he thought.

—*For a turncoat!* He heard a voice inside telling him.

A branch that moved scared him and made him fall down. He looked around with an angry glance. Who said that word? He'd rush over to him and tear him apart! Who dared to say that? So, yes! He was a turncoat! He was an apostate!

"Are you a Christian? Because if you are, you'll become a slave again!" an old friend had asked him when the decree was announced.

"Who me? Me?" he had replied and felt his face becoming like dust and ashes, and his whole body collapsing.

"Didn't your master, who is a Christian, free you?"

Oh, no! Ursus loved himself. He wouldn't put himself back into slavery. The decree was pretty clear. Freed slaves would become slaves again if they held onto their Christian faith. But he, he would never become one again.…

"He is one! I know him!" another soldier interrupted the conversation. "Come on! Admit it! Aren't you a Christian?"

He found himself in a situation of the highest danger.

What should he do? Destroy himself, just like that, without any reason? And thus he had pronounced those tiny, ugly words—the words of denial.

"No, I am not."

It seemed to him that suddenly a huge abyss opened in front of his very eyes, pitch black and horrific. And when later he would hear about the arrest of a Christian and about his or her heroic confession, Ursus would feel the sharpness of his decline even more, making him unbearably miserable.

For almost no reason he would suddenly become angry, threatening, ready for any and every evil.

He himself realized that he had become unrecognizable. Each fall brought another one, and still another one—a snowball effect of falls and evils. Oh, what a terrible thing it was to be aware of his own decline! To know that once he had been clean, a spiritual fighter and winner! And that now, alas, he was an unclean person, a coward, a lowly nothing, and so far away from God!

He shook his head to chase away the bitter thoughts. He decided to go to the city to see others like himself and be consoled. Of course, he could not be sure that he would meet someone in precisely his sorry state, but he wanted to hope....

He had not yet even put his hand on the latch of the door when the sound of footsteps on the street made him go and hide in the bushes again. But the footsteps came close to the door. He heard a hurried signal-whisper from his friend, Gaeus.

"What are you staring at?" Gaeus said when he saw him. "Come and help. The palace is on fire!"

"Fire? Who set the fire?"

Gaeus bent down and whispered into Ursus' ear that, according to Caesar Galerius, the fire had been set by the Christians. Ursus tried to protest, but Gaeus got angry and threatened to kick him out of his hut and turn him in. All Ursus' fears surfaced and drained every protest from his lips, shutting down his conscience.

Besides, how could he know? Maybe ... maybe what Gaeus had said really could have happened? Gaeus had relatives, people who were close to Galerius, and for Galerius to say things like that meant that he had some information. How could Ursus know? He wouldn't be responsible. He would just repeat what the others had said—whatever his friend told him. He wouldn't be responsible!

At the marketplace the crowds were talking in groups with loud voices and gestures about the odd and worrisome event. It was the second time in a few days that a fire had been set in one of the palace apartments, and this could have bad consequences for everyone. Who was setting these fires?

"Who's setting the fires?" someone asked.

"Who? What a question, as if you didn't know! The Christians are doing it!" said a hoarse voice, as if coming from out of Hades. "The Christians!"

"Really?" a middle-aged trader with a kind face cried with surprise.

"What do you mean, 'really?' Hmph! Yes, the Christians are setting fires!" the speaker said, then stopped to take a breath and continued with even more hatred. "The Christians *are* fire.... They are like fire that melts gold, that tortures people.... The Christians are fire and set fire wherever they pass! They set fires!... Fires!"

The crowd was listening dumbfounded to this out-of-control passerby, with his eyes bulging wide and his lips yellow and snarling, his face full of sweat that dripped with agony and hatred.

It was Ursus!

To provoke their spirits to anger, and to justify the persecution that would soon become even harsher, someone had to spread this slander to the people. And the betrayer was capable of doing even that, too.

So what if the Emperor did not have proof against so many innocent people? He had parchments all over his fine imperial desk, the one decorated with ivory and emeralds. He could easily write inhuman decrees, powerful decrees, effective decrees that would annihilate the proud army of Christians who refused to worship him as a god. These decrees would erase Christianity from the face of the earth forever!

In a short time, two more decrees were announced after the first one, threatening the officers and functionaries who did not apply them effectively so as to create the greatest triumph for their almighty master. Christians from all the cities of the Empire would have to undergo strict interrogation and would be obliged to make burnt offerings to the gods, the first decree ruled; while the second one prescribed the harshest tortures for those who did not obey. The Emperor's triumph was certain. Who would dare not to comply? On the contrary, which of the people loyal to him would lack the ambition to help him in this great work, so as to attract his favor?

Ursus would sleep with nightmares and wake up with fears. He couldn't stand to look at the sky. He couldn't look down at the earth. He couldn't stand to see another human glance. Neither pagan nor Jew nor Chr... no! Not that word! He would never again even think their name! He felt that everything and everyone on earth was calling him the same terrifying, unbearable word:

The traitor!

The traitor!

The traitor!

The whole universe was echoing that grating, torturing sound....

There were times—for a few seconds or a few moments—that even in his anguish and guilt Ursus would distinguish a soft paternal voice consoling him, affectionate hands wiping his forehead, a glance that did not regard him with disgust.

"You have fallen, Ursus!" he would think he heard. *"You've fallen a long way.... But sweet repentance erases everything. It gives you back His mercy. Why are you delaying? Why are you delaying, Ursus?"*

What?

To go to the priest and confess to the Christians that he was a betrayer, maybe the only one, while they were strong and intrepid? Shame would drown him! His dignity would vanish. His whole self-esteem would vanish. No! He couldn't do that, he couldn't lay down his pride. Besides, what kind of dangers would surround him after such a confession? What threats?

"Never, never!"

So Ursus remained hard, wild, unrepentant, preferring the eternally torturing echo to the relief of a humble confession. The renegade! The betrayer!

Of course, Gaeus was pleased with him. He had told him so in the most flattering way the other day, over at the wine-shop in front of everybody. And moreover, he reminded him to pay attention to his future so as to have the Emperor's favor. He suggested that, by pressing charges against two or three Christians, Ursus would ensure his continued freedom.

"That shouldn't be difficult. I'm sure you know plenty of them!" Gaeus concluded. "Ha, Ha! You're not going to be afraid of them, are you?"

"Who me? Afraid?" Ursus said, stammering and showing that he wanted to drop the subject.

To bring charges against the Christians?—he would never go that far, he thought. From now on he would just forget about everybody. He would ignore them. He would only concentrate on his job. He would tell Gaeus to leave him alone once and for all....

But he wouldn't say it here, in the presence of so many people. He had to find the right timing. He would say it another time.

"Poor Ursus! Do you really think that the small good decision growing now in your heart can be postponed without fading and dying?" he again heard the soft voice saying inside him.

But he paid no attention to it. The time of temptation had come, and the inner protest that he "would never go that far" was already forgotten.

How could he hide the fact that he was envious of Adrian, his former master, who had given him his freedom? As much as he tried to conceal this envy of him, there were times in which he would show it in one way or another, to either a servant or a neighbor.

Why should Adrian be rich and he poor?

Why should Adrian be free and he born into slavery?

Even when his young master (Adrian had just turned twenty-seven) had called him with his face full of happiness and had given him the signed document granting him his freedom, Ursus thought that Adrian was also obliged to give him a large sum of money so that he could move into the job that Adrian had found for him. And of course he did not think of this as a sign of ingratitude. Why had Adrian not thought then about his responsibility? But he would pay for it now, and this time whether he wanted to or not! Gaeus was right. He should pay attention to his future. He would do it.

He chose a time in the afternoon, when the traffic in the streets of Nicomedia was slow. He was walking ahead of the soldiers so that no one would be suspicious, his gait irregular and his face pale as wax. So as to completely get away with his betrayal and to avoid suspicion, he would not attack Adrian directly. The result would be all the same for him if they arrested Natalia instead.

When he reached the turn of the road, he waited for the soldiers to come close and, pointing his finger towards the door of the house that for so many years had given him love and hospitality, he said, "That door! The mistress of the house is a Christian!"

Then, as if all the panthers of the earth were chasing him, he started running like a crazy man without even looking where he was going, without knowing who he was or what he was doing. He only knew one thing: that he was the betrayer ... the apostate.

Was it in his dizziness that he had made a mistake? Or maybe the soldiers had not understood where he was pointing. It didn't matter anyway. Where there were guilty ones, they would find them.

The soldiers walked quietly, reaching the house of Urvinos. They went up the stairs and started banging wildly at the door of the home neighboring Adrian's!

5

MOM, A CHRISTIAN!

As pale as her white robe, with her hair disheveled, her eyes red, and her face soaked with tears, Pavla reached the gym, weak and about to faint. She begged the doorman to find her brother, and when she saw him coming close to her at last, with his face frowning over her unprecedented boldness at interrupting his training, she burst into a loud and poignant cry: "Why are you standing there, Helianos? They ... arrested ... Mom!" she hardly managed to say and then broke into sobs again.

He stared at her, feeling his eyes getting watery.

"What did you say?"

"The soldiers! They ... took her ... with them. She kissed us for the last time!..."

Helianos felt like hitting her. He thought that she was just acting and kidding with him.

"They ... they called her ... a Christian!" Pavla continued with her face in her palms.

"A Christian!" Helianos roared. "And why didn't anybody say something? Why didn't she say something to prove them liars? Their foul slander!"

Pavla burst out in a louder sob.

"Why didn't you say something, you coward? You're unworthy to defend your own mother!"

"They didn't believe us ... because she ... because she said she is!"

"She said she is what?"

"That she is a Christian!"

Helianos was up to his throat with anger. It seemed to him that suddenly the sun was blotted out, that the world was gone, and that everything was drowning in a huge lake with the name "Desperation."

He began running toward their home. If he could just catch up with the soldiers, maybe he could persuade her to take back what she had said and he could bribe the soldiers with some silver coins to turn back and forget the whole incident.

His father had been away in Chalcedon on business for the store, and would not return home until late in the evening. By that time it would be too late to do anything. His mother's salvation depended on him!

"Where are they?!" he said with a loud, angry voice as he entered the house. "Where are they?!"

The deadly silence that reigned throughout the house, the red eyes, the pale faces answered back what their tongues could not utter.

"Why didn't you call me?! Huh?! Why?!" he shouted and gave a hard slap in the face to one of the servants who was nearby. "Why didn't you call General Teaos to vouch for her?!"

He didn't know what he was saying. He went through all the rooms, looking with insatiable eyes for some hope, any kind of evidence that what he was going through was just a dream.

He asked again and again for them to tell him the details

of that terrible moment, and he threatened the betrayer, whoever it was, with unmerciful revenge. Putting on his good robe, he got ready to go out.

"Where are you going?" Pavla dared to ask softly, while Antiochos, paler than ever, looked at him with frightened eyes.

Grandpa, sitting on a stool, would not raise his head, and little Ione in the arms of Kyrianna looked like a frightened bird that had lost her voice.

"Where am I going? Wherever I can!" he answered, trying to hide a sob.

He opened the door and went out.

As he was walking through the streets with his head bent, drowned in his own piteous thoughts, he almost ran into the javelin of a soldier who was passing by. The soldier gave him a hard shove and angrily ordered him to stay away.

That is when Helianos came to his senses and looked around him. The army detachment that he saw filled him with shock, but also with hope. *Was she there?* Was his sweet mother in that cohort that was guarding everybody? If so, then he could run and fall down on his knees and beg her to come back to them. He could go and beg the officer to wait so that he could go and bring the documents declaring her freedom.

He let his insatiable eyes look around. *Was she there?* No.

Various unknown faces were passing by before him. And they were all young faces: children, and many teenagers like him. How many were there? He did not have the time to count them all, but his surprise made him take notice and guess their number. There were probably eighty of them....

"Amazing! Eighty-four* young men," whispered someone nearby, who was also experiencing the same surprise.

"Where are they taking them?" Helianos asked.

"What? Where are they taking them? They're Christians!" a third one answered.

"It's the whole Academy of Babylas,"* a woman added. "First they arrested the professor and then they threatened the boys. But none of them would deny they were Christians.... Oh, who knows how many mothers are going to mourn!"

"And how many kids are already mourning!" Helianos sighed with trembling lips.

Suddenly a young face known to him turned toward him and smiled at him while passing by. A hand waved, bidding him a soft farewell.

"Rhodon!" Helianos burst out and ran up to him. "Rhodon, why don't you deny it? Why do you destroy yourself? Don't you think of your mother? Don't you realize that you're leaving her alone and deserted? Say, Rhodon, confess your mistake and the Emperor will forgive you!"

Helianos spoke to him with a voice irritated and broken with emotion, as if he were talking to his own mother. This time the soldier did not kick him away, because Helianos was doing well in helping them with their job.

"Recant, Rhodon, and I will have a way to help you," he insisted, holding his hand.

"If you only knew, if you only *wanted* to know, Helianos, what you are asking me to deny, you would never say that! From the bottom of my heart, I hope you'll learn someday," he answered thoughtfully, looking him straight in the eyes.

A sudden slap in Rhodon's face made him stop speaking. An angry soldier ordered them all to increase their pace. The imperial generosity did not have patience with those who despised its leniency. The two old friends would be separated forever. Their ways were so different.

Rhodon had fulfilled his mission well the night before. Galloping speedily on his horse, he managed to reach Adrian's countryside villa around midnight and helped the brothers secure all their books. Well-sealed copper trunks were buried in newly dug dens, far away from the villa and close to the fields, in order to protect their precious contents. For this reason, the Examiner who arrived there the following day, knowing what had been going on at the villa before the persecutions, found neither books nor people. Yes, Rhodon had executed his mission well.

Earlier, Helianos had heard with gladness and a sense of relief that Rhodon was still alive, and that he had not been in the Christians' church that morning. It was not impossible either, he thought with satisfaction, that his friend had listened to his advice and changed his mind. In the meantime he had not had a chance to meet up with him, and so he stayed with those thoughts. But then on seeing him again today under those conditions, yet still with the same resolve and perseverance, Helianos felt hardness grip his heart all over again.

"So they all deserve what they get!" he mumbled as he continued his way to the house of General Teaos, trying to forget about Rhodon....

The General was not there yet, but they told him that he would not be long. As the time for their journey was close at hand, he was arranging all his business and receiving his orders for his future responsibilities. Alexandria would be their first stop.

The son of Urvinos was well known to the Teaos family,

and he was therefore escorted to the spacious living room where some visitors were chatting.

Full of shame because of the disgrace that had happened in their family, Helianos had come to ask the General for his mother's release. Maybe she had been converted against her will. Maybe she did not even understand what the soldiers were asking her and was but a victim by mistake. They had to help save her! And Teaos had a good chance to succeed in this, being as close as he was to Empress Alexandra and even directly to Diocletian.

He sat down on the edge of a sofa. The family dog was sleeping on some sheepskin by the fireplace, and he began to caress his hairy head with the long floppy ears. The dog half opened his eyes and wagged his tail happily, showing that he had not forgotten his previous contact with the boy.

Helianos focused his attention on a huge sea shell that was standing on a tripod. The light green, pink and silver lines on the inside surface had a unique glisten that came together in harmonious opposition, as if they had been pulled together by the hand of a great painter. On the curved outside, large and small thorn-like ledges of pale white and mother-of-pearl seemed to be telling him about the treasures that the ocean held inside, in places far, far away.

He did not want to sit close to the visitors, but instead wanted to stay away in case someone asked him about his family or perhaps opened a conversation about the calamity of the persecutions in which they now found themselves. But when a certain sentence came to his ears, it absorbed all his attention.

"Did you hear? Pantoleon is a Christian!"

"Pantoleon[1] who? The doctor?"

"Yes, indeed! The doctor!"

"Really?!"

"I had my suspicions! Since they freed all their slaves and forgave all the debts that people owed to Efstorgios, his father, I knew that something had changed in that household!"

"But he was a great doctor!"

"You tell me! He saved me twice from death due to an epidemic."

"Don't forget about how many poor people he treated for free! That blind guy who lived by the market, they said he regained his sight because of Pantoleon's therapy."

"Not with therapy! With a prayer, they said, that Pantoleon made to their God. Like that time he brought back to life that dead kid in the street, who had been bitten by a poisonous snake. That blind guy who regained his sight was actually the reason that everybody found out what the doctor believed in."

"I heard that he never hesitated to reveal his faith. Any house he visited, he would always talk about their teachings."

"Then he deserved to be punished! Did they arrest him?"

"It's a shame! Such a great guy! It's a shame for Nicomedia to lose such a great doctor. Do you think they only arrested him? No, sir! The Emperor himself ordered his soldiers to bring him in front of him so that he could convince him to change his mind and confess that all his miraculous cures were performed by the power of the god Asklepios. But nothing happened. So he ordered them to torture him brutally. They tore him to pieces with iron nails,

---

1. "Pantoleon" was the original name of the holy great martyr Saint Panteleimon.—Ed.

they burnt him with lit torches, they threw him in a pot of boiling oil. And I heard that the strange thing about it was that, after all those tortures, he would appear again the next day, strong and unharmed! Now they are planning to throw him to the wild beasts in the stadium. Pantoleon won't be alive for much longer!"

Helianos was listening and holding his breath. Not only did he know Pantoleon, but he also admired him deeply. He would never forget the joy and gratitude his whole family had felt that time when Antiochos had been in danger. Many doctors were coming and going in their house, getting paid well but finding no cure for Antiochos. Pantoleon examined him carefully and then, raising his handsome face from the sick child, he smiled and said to them in a sweet voice that made everyone's lost hopes revive, "We are going to make him well!"

And with his care, in only a few days Antiochos was fine and out of bed.

So, this brilliant young doctor, this superb man, the one who was so famous and so educated, was a *Christian?* Was this possible?

The General's arrival interrupted the conversations in the living room and filled Helianos with anticipation. The unbearable shame that he had felt about his mother a little while before was somehow alleviated. After all, even Pantoleon was a Christian!

"Get lost, all of you! Everybody get out of my sight! I don't want to see anybody again.... The happiness of my home is gone! My name is libeled forever...."

Urvinos was running around the house like a wounded lion, angry and unrestrainable, crazed by his anger. He was banging the doors, throwing the chairs, opening up and emptying the closets and the cabinets, trying to discover something, anything, that would prove the guilt—something that would show that there had been signs of the calamity around him, but that they had gone unnoticed and unpunished by him.

He yelled at little Ione, who was crying quietly, and he threatened to punish Pavla, who was closer to her mother than all the rest, because she had not realized the catastrophe that was happening in their home.

It was not only sadness that had overcome him when he had arrived home that night and learned the news. It was also anger over the insult, over the contempt that his wife had shown to his name.

Who would take him seriously again in society? Who would greet him, knowing that this humiliating heresy of the Christians, which was being persecuted with so many imperial decrees, had made inroads even into his own house?

It would be better for a fire to burn him inch by inch, better for the house to be torn down stone by stone, than to have this shame covering him.

There was only one thing that he could do to keep his honor, to save his self-esteem. Only one thing ...

Urvinos' mind was working the whole night through, as he stayed awake thinking about it. In the morning, before he left for the store, he took Helianos to the side and told him bluntly, "We will denounce her! You will sign papers saying that you don't recognize her as your mother anymore! No person who disrespects the laws of the Emperor belongs to our family! Do you get it? Otherwise both my future and yours are gone!"

His eyes, red from insomnia, were throwing flames and his face was frightening. How could his son talk back to him and suggest another course of action? Besides, yesterday General Teaos had seemed very hesitant to try to obtain Tatiani's release.

The Emperor was outraged seeing that the decrees that he, Gaios Avrilios Valerios Diocletian, the unconquerable Sevastos, the High Priest, the Supreme Ruler of the Germans, the King of the Egyptians—that he, the Father of the country, had signed, did not create even the slightest fear among the Christians!

Had not one of them torn apart the decree once it had been posted in the main square of Nicomedia? And that person was a high government official on top of that! Then Anikitos* had dared to tell him, the Emperor, right to his face and in front of the Senators, that he had fallen into error by applying such measures against the Christians, who were the most peaceful and gentle citizens of his empire! Bless Galerius, who was near him at the time and had advised him to judge the impudent one strictly.

So what if his plans to set an example by torturing Anikitos had not gone exactly the way he had wanted? So what if they had thrown him to the hungry lion in the stadium and it had not even come close to him? It did not even matter that when they had tied him to the wheel and made him pass through fire, the flames had been mysteriously extinguished. Now he was going to rot in jail along with his nephew Fotios,* who, influenced by witnessing his uncle's torture, had confessed that he too was a Christian.

And there were more officials—the members of the Senate, Hindis* and Gorgonios,* and Peter* and General Zenon* and Commander Dorotheos,* and a crowd of people who chose the most horrible tortures rather than to do his will. The Emperor was infuriated.

Teaos thought that it would be risky to ask for a favor for a woman who had been sentenced under the law. But at the same time he thought that perhaps Diocletian might not deny his request, in order to secure the loyalty of his future attendant by this show of kindness. His very obvious hesitancy filled Helianos with shame once again. It also filled him with fear. His father was right that they should think about their future. They should worry that they would lose everything. Instead, with the solution they had come up with, as tough as it was, they would stand to gain a lot. They would gain everything!…

Ione, who had just been lifted out of her cradle, with her uncombed hair turning back in small curls, put her head behind a high chair at the end of the hall and smiled at him as always. Then she came close to him, and pulling his robe she said to him half crying, "Mommy … Where is Mommy?"

He was shocked. He was ashamed to look his baby sister in the eyes. He shook his head and left to hide a sob. He ran inside the first doorway that he came to.

Was it a coincidence? Or had he already started to go there before his father had stopped him? He shivered. He was in his mother's workshop.

All of her things were neatly put together, testifying to Tatiani's tidiness and to her affectionate care for everyone. On the sofa, a robe that belonged to him was left where she had been sewing a new stripe with gold and red thread, proving that he had been the last thing on her mind. A deep emotion seized him.

He started looking through her things, touching them with tender respect, trying to find something that would reveal her beliefs which had been so well hidden—something that would prove to him that she really was a Christian.

But Helianos did not find anything. Only the well-closed locks of the rosewood trunk attracted his attention and prompted him to look there. It took him a while to pry off the nails, and when he finally did open the trunk he saw only fabrics lying there neatly. He was about to close the wooden top, when something made him put his hands into the material and grope around inside. And then …

One … two … three parchments made him shiver as his hands touched them. He knelt in front of the trunk and started taking out all those endless papyrus scrolls and parchments with the Christian texts, staring at them, pale, tight-lipped and fiery-eyed.

So, the Emperor's soldiers were right. Here was the evidence, the most persuasive of all the accusations that anyone could have made! Here was the reason for the catastrophe that had befallen his mother, who had preferred them to the happiness of her family.

His father was right. Yes, he was.... They should denounce her.

He untied one of the red ribbons that Natalia had put around the papyruses and glanced at the paper full of anger and hatred, but at the same time with an uncontrollable curiosity. What was in these papers that made them so powerful as to allure the hearts of so many people?

He sat there for a long while reading without understanding very much. But when he came across some sentences that had been written especially for his mother, he again felt overcome with emotion.

"Then they will deliver you into calamities … and you will be hated by all nations because of My name.…"

"And a man's enemies will be those of his own household.…"

A man's enemies! Helianos thought. So here was the prophecy that could apply to her situation. "And a man's enemies will be those of his own household.…"

Now she would learn in the horror of the dark prison, in the pains of her whipping, in her unbearable misfortune and surrounded by so many enemies, that first among them was … Helianos.

Her Helianos! Her tough and implacable enemy. A wrenching sob came from the depths of his heart. He put his head in his palms, still holding the papyrus, and broke down in tears there at the edge of the sofa.

When he raised his head up and looked for the piteous sentence, "And a man's enemies will be those of his own household …," he saw that his tears had washed away part of it. He felt relieved.

"I'll do anything to save you, my dear Mother!" he whispered to himself, and opened more papyruses in order to read zealously the things that she had been reading.

A knock at the front door made him throw all the papyruses back in the trunk and quickly cover them up with some textiles. When he went to unlock the door, nothing was left behind him to show that in the little workshop a priceless fortune was hidden, more expensive by any comparison than the luxurious textiles and silks.

Pavla, wearing a dark tunic and with a long shawl thrown over her head, entered the house.

"I'm going to see Mom!" she told him, distraught.

"Where are you going? Do you know where they are holding her?"

"I don't know. I'll go and ask at all the prisons. I'll beg them to allow me to see her, and I'll try to convince her to change! We have to do it! We don't know what's happening from one day to the next."

He looked at her undecidedly: "Are you going alone?"

"Yes, alone!"

"Go, Pavla! Go…. Only, if you manage to see her, don't speak to her like an enemy. Only that … I … will go to the Emperor."

"To the Emperor? Do you think he will see you?"

"I want to hope that he will. And I want to be the one to take the favorable decision to her. May the gods help us. Teaos will give me an answer today from the Emperor."

As they spoke, they heard a soft signal knock at the little stained-glass window that seemed to be the wind blowing. They had no time to think, because Kyrianna told them that an Examiner wanted to search the house.

"There is nothing Christian in the house of Urvinos!" yelled Pavla, full of anger, when she saw the Examiner entering the house.

"Urvinos, the textile trader?" he asked suddenly.

"Exactly!"

"It's probably a mistake with the name," he apologized, looking at the papyrus he was holding.

Helianos bit down on his lip and kept silent. A voice was welling up from deep inside, trying to force its way out of his mouth and to say that only a few yards behind them, there in the rosewood trunk, was a pile of Christian books that had stolen their happiness and that should be destroyed. That should be thrown into fire right then and there! *Here they are! Take them! Help us make them disappear from the face of the earth forever!* The little voice screamed inside him, justified and convincing, behind his clenched teeth and lips.

But Helianos did not say a word.

Those unprotected, well-wrapped papyruses and rolls of parchment of his mother's, with the beautiful calligraphy and the incomprehensibly sweet words, would find protection from him for his mother's sake. He would never betray them!

And it seemed to him that, with this thought and this decision, their cold empty house was suddenly filled again with her presence, with the warmth that her affection poured out. He thought that her face, full of light and joy, appeared across from him and smiled at him while whispering tenderly, *"My brave boy, Helianos!"*

"Father searched the whole house and didn't find anything Christian—neither an icon[1] nor a book," Pavla added once the Examiner and his people had left.

"Why are they so against the Christian books?" her brother asked her skeptically, changing the subject.

"I don't know. Maybe because ..."

---

1. From the earliest days of the Church, Christians venerated (not worshipped) pictorial representations of the Lord Jesus Christ, the Virgin Mary, the Holy Apostles, the Saints and the Angels. The use of *icons*, some of which are miraculous, remains to the present day an essential part of the daily prayer, worship and religious education of Orthodox Christians around the world.—ED.

"Why?"

"Maybe because … they make people better.… I've heard …"

The soft knock at the stained-glass window had come from Natalia, who was not aware of her friend's arrest or of the danger in which the books remained in the fanatic idolater's house.

But her prayers, along with the prayers of so many of the Christian brothers and sisters, and the secret, fiery entreaties of the jailed Tatiani for the protection of their treasure, the word of God, were reaching His heavenly throne as fragrant incense. The prayers became like the protective wings of angels, and God spoke kind words into Tatiani's heart, which had previously not known Him so well.

Before leaving the house that morning, Helianos changed the old locks, put new nails in the trunk, and took the key of the room with him.

What would this new day bring to their home?

6

TO THE EMPEROR FOR A FAVOR

THE guards—four tall, well-built African warriors with a frightful appearance and gleaming spears—were giving them fierce looks. For the third time, General Teaos showed the pass that allowed them to enter the palace, and moved forward into the long corridor with the rose and black marble tiles.

On the right side, a large four-paneled door with carved geometrical designs implied that they were getting closer to the suite of rooms where, invisible to the people, the unapproachable monarch would hold hearings.

It was not certain whether both Teaos and Helianos would be allowed into the throne room, or if some court official would convey their demand to the Emperor. And if Teaos did not have to receive any further instructions for his confidential journey, it was not certain that he would be able to see the Emperor even by himself.

Helianos stared ecstatically around the huge room where they were led. He had never imagined so much gold and wealth, so much luxury and grandeur, with which the imperial palace was decorated inside.

A vast hall with an extremely high gold ceiling was dressed with expensive Persian rugs on its marble floor and handwoven silk tapestries on the walls. Hand-carved, solid marble benches and exceptional statues and sculptured busts were spread out on golden tripods within the room where fragrant incense was burning.

A velvety dark red curtain with countless pleats was held fast to the two sides of the doorframe with golden tasseled cords, revealing the even more luxurious throne room on the other side of it.

A double line of colonnades with exquisite golden capitals supported the throne room on the right and left sides. A platform, consisting of three wide marble stairs and ending in a large landing covered with a rug, allowed a carved marble chair to stand out in the center of the room's east side. On top of the pedestal, a purple-colored pillow was placed on the high-backed imperial throne, which was covered with leaves of pure gold.

Big gold-embroidered pillows on the bottom and the sides of the seat made it a comfortable place for the great sovereign master, while the two round spheres on the handles of his throne reminded him that his sovereignty extended all around the world.

Behind his throne were seats for his exceptional bodyguards, whose excellent physical presence made the majestic scene even more spectacular. Their breastplates and helmets shimmered. Their distinguishing epaulettes and their military belts of honor sparkled, and the points of their upright javelins glittered with the slightest motion. The Emperor had not yet arrived.

Helianos felt that he was dreaming. All his problems seemed to vanish and he almost forgot the reason he was there.

Before him was only this phantasmagoric view of wealth,

power and glory! His great career expectations instantly came back to life! He saw himself first somewhere there behind the throne, shining in one of those uniforms. Then he saw himself in the place of one of those great warrior-generals.... *Who was the famed George before?* he thought. *Who was Constantine?...* And then he even dared to see himself, a few years later, as the Emp ...

A commotion in the throne room suddenly brought him back to reality. The Chief of the Imperial Guard entered full of anger, barked out some orders and scattered threats, then left. Then he came back in and seemed to have something very serious to announce to the Emperor.

When he saw General Teaos, he walked over to him and whispered something secretly, with desperate gesticulation and an obvious sadness.

"Curses!" Teaos let out, unable to hold back his surprise. "Oh, thunderbolt! Oh, gods!" he cried out, raising up his hands. "When are you going to crush this ungodly heresy with your powers? Did you allow it to come even to this holy palace?"

The Chief of the Imperial Guard made a sign for him not to speak so loudly. Teaos sat on one of the marble benches covered with a leopard skin and hit his palms on his knees with desperation.

"George?" he whispered. "George? Oh, gods! Is it possible? Tell me!..."

Who would answer back? And who would prove false what the Chief of the Imperial Guard had seen and heard with his own eyes? As unable as he felt to digest the news, as terrible an affliction as he felt, this was not a nightmare! And even if he felt for a moment that this was just a bad dream, reality woke him up and shook him. What should he tell the Emperor? How could he tell him that Count George, with his unique presence and beauty, with his intelligence and education, with his good judgment and strong will—Count George, the brave one with his many military exploits (had it not been just a little while before that he had shown incredible heroism in the war with the Persians?)—Count George, the famed, the special, the Emperor's beloved—had appeared a little while ago before him and confessed?…

"Yes," explained the Chief, "he stated it seriously and irrevocably, that all the decrees of the persecution against the Christians should be put into effect against him, too."

When George had stated this, the Chief had yelled back thunderstruck, "'What are you talking about, glorious Count? Take back what you just said. Forget it, I beg of you! Do not deprive the Empire of your brave service. Recant your confession, and I'll forget it too!'"

But George could not be persuaded. Rumors had spread, saying that after the death of his mother, during his short leave in Lydda, her homeland, he had sold all of her land and given most of the money to the needy people there. And when he returned to Nicomedia, no one ever found out where the rest of his inheritance had gone.

Did these things have anything to do with his statement? Had this been a sort of preparation for his actual protest against the persecution? Who knew? The fact was that George was no longer a superior officer, no longer a Count of the Imperial Guard. How could Diocletian stand to hear this unbearable confession? And what kind of consequences would it have for the rest of them?

That was why the Chief of the Imperial Guard had gone

back and forth, in and out of the hall, shouting threats at everyone.

Teaos stood up abruptly. A thought filled him with concern. He approached the Chief and asked him not to announce Count George's case first, but to allow him to speak first to the Emperor about his matter; otherwise all their hopes could be dashed—even those concerning their upcoming journey!

Suddenly, at that very moment, two servants went over to the open curtains, which had allowed Teaos and Helianos to get a good view of the throne room during the time they had been there, and pulled them closed. It was time for the Emperor to arrive. The courtiers took their positions. The senators of the states and the delegates who came from Rome moved forward and waited for their turn to be heard.

Then everything happened so quickly. Helianos did not even realize when their turn came. When Teaos went into the throne room and mentioned to Diocletian his future military attaché's petition about his mother, Diocletian asked to see Helianos in person.

Helianos came before the Emperor, who did not seem unpleasant. While Helianos was bent down, kneeling in front of the purple-cushioned footstool, where the Emperor's feet were resting in their tall pearl covered sandals, with a start he heard the Emperor's hoarse voice saying, "She is free...."

The Emperor paused for a second and then continued, "She is free, of course, from the time that you convince her to change her ideas! I will expect you to do so!"

Helianos thanked him emotionally. With confidence he thought that the Emperor's condition was easy to fulfill. He exited the throne room and in a few minutes he was out of the palace, following the General and feeling a bit dazed. It seemed that he had just come out of a wonderful dream—a dream full of the great promises that he had heard and all the wonders that he had seen.

After they had walked enough and were sitting in their enclosed carriage, Helianos remembered to ask the General for the answer to the question that had arisen so intensely inside of him a little earlier.

"What happened to George, General?"

He imagined yet another of the Count's heroic acts that had filled the army with enthusiasm, creating a new triumph and glory, and probably even causing the Emperor to worry about his position. Was that what was happening?

"You didn't hear?" shouted Teaos, coming out of his deep thoughts with exasperation. "You didn't hear?"

"No, sir! I couldn't hear your conversation."

"Count George confessed that he's a Christian!"

"What?! Count George is a Christian, too?"

Helianos looked at him as if he had not understood. He really thought that he must not have heard the General's reply properly.

Returning home, Helianos waited for Pavla's news. Had she managed to meet their mother, or had she waited outside the closed doors of the prison in vain, as she had earlier this morning?

He would have preferred the latter, if anyone had asked. In his inner thoughts, he was afraid that if his mother refused to change her faith for his sister, then obviously she would refuse to do it for him as well. But he would bring up so many arguments, so many convincing words, so many supplications, that he was certain she would not insist on keeping her ideas. But the last thing he wanted was for her to give his sister an answer that would make it even harder for her to change her mind, before he had a chance to make his pleas.

Tomorrow he and Pavla would have written permission to enter the prison freely, in order to visit her and stay there as long as it would take them to convince her and bring her back home, free forever! A joy filled him with a certain fledgling hope. But he also had other thoughts. Now he would be able to talk to his father and tell him that he should wait patiently for his mother to come back. And of course his father would not be able to find a reason to resist.

With the key that he carried with him, he quietly opened his mother's workshop. Did he want to take that robe with the unfinished chevron? Or perhaps he wanted to be close to those papyruses, to read them and then recite a few words from them to his mother to touch her even more? Actually he wanted both.

As he entered the room, a small papyrus roll tightly tied together on the floor drew his attention. He was absolutely sure that he had locked everything up well in the trunk that morning. He had looked around all the corners to be sure he had not missed anything. He had looked behind the sofas and in the sewing baskets. And before he left and locked the door he had even taken a last glance around the whole room, just to be on the safe side. But how had this piece of paper come to be on the floor? He picked it up with surprise and read it with fear.

There were only two sentences, which read: "They have arrested him. Pray that he will not renounce the faith."

Gods! Who had thrown this paper into the room? And from where? The slit of the door was very narrow and the window was locked. Whose hand had written this? And to whom was it addressed?

He felt a light sweat covering his face. Was this a kind of miraculous act in order to force him to abandon his plans? "Pray that he will not renounce the faith." Obviously this phrase was written by a Christian for a Christian. Was this written for his mother so as to encourage her and strengthen her desire to "not renounce the faith"? What would come of all his convincing arguments? What about the Emperor's condition? All his joy faded with these thoughts.

And since it was certain that this note was intended for a Christian, finding it in their home meant that maybe there was someone else. Oh, what would happen if such a suspicion entered into his father's mind? He would throw everybody out!

But who could it be, since his grandfather and all the servants would dutifully put incense before the statues of the household gods every day? His brother and sisters? Impossible! And of course his father was not a Christian. Neither was he! Who then could it be?

He took the papyrus and ripped it up into a hundred pieces. This handwriting did not even resemble his mother's handwriting.

Pavla's return made him almost forget about this incident. Her second visit to the prison had not produced any results. The same guard who that very morning had given her some hope of seeing their mother now had much stricter orders and was completely inflexible.

"At that same time, they were bringing in a new convict

with a big military escort, and everybody was upset and agitated. He seemed to be very official," she added sadly.

"Was he young?"

"Yes."

"Tall?"

"Yes."

"It was probably Count George!" Helianos whispered and felt his knees paralyzed.

Following the news about the doctor, Pantoleon, now Count George also turned out to be a Christian! How could such horrible things be happening for real? Gods! If this was in fact true, would it prove to be an obstacle to the fulfillment of his own great dream?

7

GRIEF AND JOY

L ARGE noble houses not only embellish a city with their aesthetic beauty but they also perform a beneficial social function when they are in good hands. That is what everyone thought when they knocked at Natalia's door. The door-woman who opened the door indicated with her gentle smile that her master and mistress welcomed everyone in the same polite way, and that their hearts, full of love, would always find something to comfort and to please their visitors.

Especially now that so much grief had spread throughout Nicomedia as a result of the persecutions, Adrian's and Natalia's house had become a shelter for the widows of the martyrs and a warm nest for their orphaned children. For in most cases these poor wretches had lost not only their protectors and their parents but also their property.

The people loyal to the Emperor were determined to increase the wealth and the income of his realm every day by confiscating the property of the Christians. The share of the spoils that was offered to every betrayer became a catalyst for new charges and further confiscation, and this reward was evidently not so unpleasant for them.

The Christian Church, with its maternal love and compassion for all, tried to respond to the pressing needs of many. The remaining faithful eagerly decided to help their brethren with great monetary sacrifices. Adrian's country villa sheltered many widows and their children, and his noble house in the center of the city was also a relief to many. Much of the money that was being collected from the community of the faithful was distributed there. And the food that was prepared was always a lot more than was needed for Adrian and Natalia and their staff.

That evening Natalia and two of her friends were making a new list of the needy to whom they would distribute the new donations. As much as they had tried to keep it a secret, it was widely rumored that on coming back from Lydda Count George had given the Church a very significant amount of money. And indeed there was no reason for them to doubt that the donations handed over to them today by the priest, Nikandros, had come from him.

As the list was being compiled, some children sitting on a narrow bench in the windowless corridor were chanting in sweet voices, "*I shall love Thee, O Lord, my Power. The Lord is my Strength, my Shelter and my Savior.*"

Their chanting echoed through the house, filling everyone's heart with peace. These were great days! Their faith was so strong! The feeling that God was near them, with them—that He was their Power, their Strength, their Shelter and their Savior—was reflected on the shiny faces of the young and the old alike. Their hearts were at peace. Happiness and joy were not a past reality for them; they were present here and now, today! And deeply, permanently!

Indeed, perhaps just outside the door the most terrible, most severe persecution in the history of the Church was raging. There were the examining magistrates, the tyrants, the executioners, the horrible instruments of torture, the amphitheater, the wild beasts … death. They were real, they were threatening, and they were so close at hand…. But all those horrors were out there, outside of the door of their souls. Inside, the sweetest peace reigned. Martyrdom was not pain for the faithful. It was glory! It was a wreath! It was the opening of Heaven, the spiritual gift of endless joy!

How could the faithful not feel joy, looking around at the many heroes who, through their deaths, had glorified their King and God? These martyrs had proved that their faith in Him was their greatest treasure and that their love for Him had overcome their love for their own lives. Fire might burn their bodies, the torturing wheels and the iron nails might rip up their ribs, the beasts and the deadly lashings might tear their flesh to pieces, but nothing could reach their hearts and their souls. They were intact, mighty and powerful! They were able not only to endure but to be gladdened. They were able not only to proclaim their faith but to rejoice in all their sufferings. They were able to live in the blissfulness of eternity even in the dark prisons and in the very places of their martyrdom.

Great days for the Christians were these, the days of persecution! The Church was alone, persecuted, drowning in her own blood, but triumphant! Deprived of any political power and protection, she was shown to be almighty and indomitable. The deaths of millions of her children gave her new life, multiplied the numbers of the faithful, and would ultimately crown her with such a glory that it would abide throughout the centuries. The Church knew that she was pleasing her Master. What greater joy could she ever ask for?

Natalia and her friends had just finished the list of the needy and were now preparing the new tunics for the children, when they received shocking news from Mertios. He told the door-woman the following:

Adrian had been present at the martyrdom of twenty-three* Christians just a while before, and he had become so enthused by their courage and the joy that shone on their faces that he had declared himself to be a Christian! Full of courage, he had started talking about the power of Christ and His Gospel to the idolaters who were standing around him. No dangers or threats had existed for him at that time. There had been only one thing in his mind: to persuade those who lived in the darkness of idolatry about the one and only Truth, his faith!

"Adrian has been arrested," Mertios continued thoughtfully. "May God be with him and with us...." Then he left hurriedly to undertake another mission.

How could Vereniki, the door-woman, break the news to Adrian's young wife? How could she tell her that she would soon become a widow, that Adrian in his youth and wealth would soon depart this world, leaving her alone?

Praying and trying to keep herself composed, Vereniki walked slowly to the room where her mistress was.

"He has been arrested?" Natalia whispered, her face and lips becoming pale.

Her eyes filled with tears. A deep pain seized her inside. But just before the tears were about to fall onto her cheeks, the faith came, along with the hope—the sweet, life-giving Christian hope—and gave her eyes a diamond-like shine. The thought came to her that Adrian would glorify the name of their Lord with his bravery, that the wreath of glory was awaiting him in Heaven. Her grief softened. Her face lightened. Her face lightened and comfort shone in her eyes. The joy!

"May God support him to the end!" she wished quietly. "All of you, please pray that he will stay faithful to the end."

This was the wish! The longing! It was the fervent desire of the faithful of those dangerous times to stay "faithful to the end," both for the faithful who were facing the examining magistrates and martyrdom at that very moment, and for themselves when their own time would come. Their only fear was that someone might renounce the faith.

Natalia wrote a little note to Tatiani, wanting to share her pain and ask for her prayers, and opening the little stained-glass window from the outside, she threw it into the workshop. She knew that no one from her friend's family ever entered her workshop, and she used this way to communicate with her whenever she did not receive an answer to her knocking at the little window. She then spoke to the children who were in her house with warm words and hurried to give them their new tunics.

It was already dark when she received a new, incomparably more horrible report. First they heard a husky voice, like the roaring of a beast, in the dark alley outside the house—a voice that muttered something, but did not make any sense other than the sound of Adrian's name.

The women held their breaths. Vereniki opened the door slightly and put her head out, frightened. Who had spoken about her brave master? What did he say? She could only see a shadow that disappeared in a hurry around the corner.

She was about to close the door when she heard the voice again. The same hoarse voice, but quite clear this time, so that they could understand what it was saying and could feel its pitiless knife ripping up their hearts.

"Adrian has recanted! Adrian will betray Christ!..." the voice said, and faded with the wind.

"What did he say?" Natalia asked with horror, not believing her own ears. "Tell me, Vereniki ... tell me what he said!"

Who could tell her? Who could repeat this awful phrase? How could this young creature with the warm, compassionate Christian heart endure this great suffering?

Rufus, who at the time was bringing the next day's supplies for the feeding of the poor, also arrived in shock. Undoubtedly he had heard the news from a little closer. Natalia questioned him persistently.

"I grabbed this guy and I asked him where he heard what he was saying," Rufus said, hesitant to continue.

"But how did he know? Did he see him with his own eyes?" she demanded.

"He said that he was present when they arrested him ... that he became afraid for his own life and that he recanted...."

"Was this man someone we know?"

"No. But I think I've seen him somewhere before."

A deadly silence unfolded right there at the entrance of the noble house. Natalia, who had not cried because of Adrian's arrest, suddenly broke down sobbing with a hopeless pain.

Helianos and Pavla, who were talking near the window overlooking the road, heard her sobs.

"Why is Natalia crying?" Pavla asked Helianos.

"Didn't you hear? She's probably Christian. And perhaps

Adrian is, too. But I just heard from somebody that Adrian will recant…. Oh! Do you think that she's the one who wrote that note that I found in mother's workshop?" he said with surprise, breaking off in the middle of his sentence, and telling his sister about the mysterious papyrus.

"So is it that bad for a Christian to recant?" Pavla whispered thoughtfully.

"Don't you start believing that nonsense, too!" Helianos yelled angrily at his sister. "It's not bad at all! Tomorrow we'll do everything in our power to convince Mom…. Her deliverance is up to us! Did you hear what I said?"

In a little while they saw Natalia running out of her house.

"Maybe she's going to try to convince him not to recant," Pavla whispered, and somehow felt shame for the dissension between the two neighboring households.

Thank goodness Helianos did not hear her.

Who could count the many suns that rose instantly in Natalia's heart? Who could uncover the many springs of joy that refreshed her inner heart and filled her with blossoms?

No! It was wrong! It was a lie! Adrian had not recanted. He was not afraid for his life!

"Deny Christ? May God have mercy upon me!" he said when Natalia finally managed to meet him and tell him about the false rumor, a little while before he was to appear before the Examiner the next morning.

He was the same intrepid and brave soul as he had been in that hour of his holy enthusiasm, when he had preached his Christ and had confessed that he was a Christian. It was all in vain that the Eparch[1] went to flatter him, and it was also in vain that his hopes arose when he saw Adrian's young wife and tried to urge her to save her husband.

Adrian remained faithful. And Natalia remained faithful. Their love for their Lord was for them their greatest happiness and joy, their greatest reward. Who had been mistaken enough to imagine that he would deny this great joy of his?...

No, Ursus had not been mistaken. As he had faced the spiritual grandeur of the joyous endurance of the twenty-three martyrs that morning, and as he had stood half-hidden behind a column and heard the brave voice of his old master preaching about Christ, he had felt the fire of malice burning through his whole being.

During that time he was living in a state of torment. Whether he was walking through the streets of Nicomedia, with its gardens and villas, or working at his job or getting ready to go to bed—at any time and in any place—as cold as it might have been outside, this fire, *his* fire could not be extinguished.

He felt that great flames were coming out of his fiery eyes, covering him up and burning his whole body and his face. Then the flames would go back into his eyes and move deeper, only to burn him more. There, they would become huge torches that would burn his heart, his entrails, his entire being.

Ursus was choking and suffering unbearably. Each and

1. An Eparch (*Eparhos*) was an appointed governing official of a local population, as in a city or province, roughly equivalent to a mayor, prefect or governor.—Ed.

every flash of the flame became a dull voice, cruel and without end, which reminded him of the time of his denial of Christ.

"You got scared, Ursus! Huh? You turned into a coward because of the pain of torture. For the spark of this short life, you preferred me! You preferred the tortures of my fire, the unending and inexorable flames. You see how sweet I am? Ha, Ha!"

It stopped for a moment, and then it started again.

"So, you are saved! You are strong, but they, the oh-so-many former brothers of yours, died hard. They are crowned as martyrs now. Your hands are safe—look at them! Your feet are safe—look how fast they walk! Your eyes only have my flames in them! As for you, you are strong! Ha! Ha! You are saved, Ursus! Ursus, betrayer and denier of your faith!"

The voice would stop, leaving the sound of sarcastic laughter, only to begin again implacable and terrifying. And he was moaning. He opened his mouth to take a breath and to refresh himself, but he was suffocating. He was dying of thirst. He, the one who was so strong and always moving—felt like a being with no life, no strength. He, who was so strong and active, felt like dry, toasted brushwood—like straw that the flames were licking, threatening from time to time with utter annihilation.

He could bear to look neither at the sky nor at the earth. He could stand to meet the look of neither idolater nor Jew nor …

Oh, that name of "Christian"! How quickly it could increase his fire! Oh, how those tortures and martyrdoms that he was hearing about and that were daily increasing in the city and in every city of the whole empire, proving that the believers were "faithful to the end"—how they were tormenting his unrepentant heart! And next to this fire of his conscience, the fire of jealousy and envy was spreading fast.

When he had found out that, by the soldiers' mistake, Natalia had not been arrested, he waited for another chance to press charges and to take his revenge. But the thought that came to his malicious mind seemed even better. *Adrian will recant!* Yes! He would shout it out loud, he would spread it. He would misinform everybody that there were others who had betrayed their faith—that he was not alone. He would bring the news first to Adrian's wife to fill her with bitterness, with deadly poison.

In the darkness his voice had come out hoarse with envy, but also from fear that someone would recognize it. The second time it had come out even wilder, and a malevolent happiness overcame him when he realized that they had heard him.

But when Natalia's sobs came to his ears, when he remembered what a terrible disaster it was for the Christians to renounce their faith and the eternal hell that it meant, his whole body trembled. Insane with fear, crazy with his guilt, and wild with anxiety, he started running, fast and insuppressibly. He turned into every street that he came across; he stumbled and slipped, always running as if the whole universe were chasing him. With his head bent as he ran, with his look extinguished by the flames of his "fire," and with his mind darkened, he fled the city and found himself in the countryside.

He was still running and running. But suddenly he felt the earth move under his feet. He had reached the edge of a cliff without realizing it. A loose rock moved from the dirt and tumbled down the gorge, dragging him along with vehemence.

"Fire!" was the only word his lips could pronounce. "Fire! Fire!"

A violent shaking followed, and then everything was over. Ursus' lips stopped forever, silently pronouncing for all time the unending eternity: *Fire!*

Some bushes moved to and fro. As they bent over the immobile body, rustling with the blowing of the wind, it seemed that they murmured with horror:

"The ungrateful one!"

"The slanderer!"

"The malicious one!"

"The betrayer!"

"… THE RENOUNCER!"

And the soil that accepted into itself the last beats of Ursus' hardened heart finished with the worst words of all:

"THE UNREPENTANT ONE!"

8

NEAR THE PRISONER

SHE stared at a little spider which was hanging from the invisible thread of its web and which slowly went down, moving its tiny feet. How could this very fine thread that could hardly be seen with the naked eye hold that weight? And how was it getting longer, so that it reached all the way from the ceiling's beam down to the floor?

She blew softly toward the spider. The spider, sensing a possible danger, turned upside down and, putting its feet together, instantly started climbing up its invisible thread again towards the ceiling to safety. Who took care of this tiny little creature and gave it a way to support and protect itself from danger? Who had armed it with a fine and unseen hand?

"Oh, Lord …"

Tatiani felt delighted at the sight of this spider and the thoughts that accompanied it. She had not been afraid for herself when they had arrested her. She had not been intimidated on going into the dank prison. Death did not scare her. What bothered her was the thought of her children.

What would happen to those tender creatures without their mother? What would happen to them, growing up without tenderness, without advice, in a household in which idolatry and delusion reigned? From the moment she had been baptized as a Christian, Tatiani had one desire burning inside her: bit-by-bit to sow in the souls of her children first some seeds of virtue, and then afterwards some seeds of Christ's truth. *In due time ...* she had thought, full of hope that someday her children would also embrace their mother's faith. What would happen now?

How could her hopes survive now? Now her hope became prayer and faith. Her Lord, Who had created this little spider with such wisdom and Who had said that not even a single sparrow would fall dead if God did not allow it, would never leave her children unprotected and deluded. She was sure about that.

The unexpected opening of the door made her turn around suddenly. A heart-rending sob, a cry issuing out of three mouths simultaneously, echoed throughout the cell and filled her eyes with tears.

"Mommy!"

Three shadows moved in the semi-darkness and fell on her, hooking themselves on her arms and her neck. Pavla and Antiochos were crying, unable to speak. Helianos, more restrained, was holding her hand and trying to get his voice back, trying to find a beginning for all the things he wanted to tell her.

"Mother, have pity on us!" he burst out finally, short of breath.

"Come back to our home, Mommy! Give it back its joy! Give it your love and your warmth! Without you everything around there is cold and dark. Please, Mommy, come back!"

"Mommy, please come back!"

"How are we going to live like this?..."

"Grandpa is going to die...."

"Ione is crying and asking for you all the time...."

The mother's heart shuddered. Helianos took fresh courage, seeing tears in her eyes.

"Mom, the Emperor granted you a favor! Please accept it, we beg of you! All your children are begging you! Accept it.... All you have to do is to recant and you'll be free!"

The Christian's heart was troubled even more.

"Deny my faith? Never! What are you asking of me, Helianos?"

"Then just say it! Just admit that you've stopped loving us, that you don't recognize us anymore!"

"I love you, my dear children, more than the treasures of this world. More than my own self. More than my own life! But not more than Christ and my soul! Oh, I regret that I didn't have a chance to teach you the priceless value of the soul! I didn't know it before. I wish for you to live and to learn! You, Helianos, who have so much love of grandeur ... Oh, if you only wanted to know!"

"Me? Me? Become a Christian? NEVER!" he said with disgust and abruptly dropped her hand.

He had something of his father's look on his face.

"As long as you are saying 'never' to renouncing, when all of us are begging for it, I am going to say 'never' to knowing your faith!" he added with obstinacy.

"If I stop saying this 'never,' I lose everything," his mother replied tenderly. "If you do, you win everything! You be the judge...."

"I do judge, and I say that a mother never puts her children through grief. She doesn't destroy their future...."

"The future is not only these few years that man lives on earth, Helianos. It is huge! It is endless! Eternal! I would like you to live in His glory, the glory of the Eternal One, you too believing in the one and only true God, the Christ and Savior of the world and of each and every human soul! He will protect you … even when I'm gone.…"

She bent and kissed Pavla and Antiochos with tenderness. Helianos jumped back.

"Come on, kids! Let's go!" he yelled, beside himself. "The guard is going to say that we are late!"

He was angry. He had become just like his father. How had he forgotten all the persuasive arguments that he was going to use to try to convince her? All those entreaties and supplications? He, who was wearing the tunic with the half-sewn chevron … he, who was going to promise her that when his ambitions were accomplished someday, he would order the end of the persecutions.… He, who was going to talk to her with so much affection, who was going to touch her and stir her emotions, was now like a stranger. Like …

"Are you not even going to say good-bye to me?" Tatiani asked with a sad smile, while her big blue eyes were already filled with tears.

Her fears for Helianos were not unjustified. She moved toward him softly. She opened her arms.

"Good-bye, my child!"

"Okay …," he cut her off abruptly and found himself close to the gate of the prison.

There was no reason to stay further. Everything was over. The second visit with Ione, whom he had left at home for another purpose, was pointless. Everything was finished.…

"You told me yesterday not to behave like an enemy to Mom," Pavla complained angrily on their way back. "And that is exactly how you behaved today!"

He suddenly recalled what he had read on the papyrus scroll: "And a man's enemies will be those of his own household." Yes, this prophecy was right. He remembered and felt shame.

He gave Pavla a threatening look and did not say a word. He only thought angrily that when they got back to the house he would throw all those papyruses—the ones that stole their mother's love from them—into the fireplace and burn them.

"How many times are we going to visit her until we convince her?" Antiochos asked thoughtfully.

"Not any more!" Helianos said stubbornly.

"And how long is the Emperor willing to wait?"

No one dared to answer back.

"I will go and visit her again!" said Antiochos resolutely.

"So will I!" agreed Pavla.

Helianos did not hear them. His father was waiting impatiently at the store for him to deliver the news to him. He was sure that nothing good would come from this meeting, and was absorbed in his thoughts.

The children separated. Antiochos turned and headed for the gym, although he was not in the mood for it, and Helianos took the main road to the market.

Pavla was going back to their home, when she felt a hand holding her with warmth.

"Pavla! How are you doing? I heard everything today! God will protect you. Don't be sad! Something good will come out of this ordeal."

It was Natalia.

Then she held her hand a little tighter, and looking her straight in the eyes she asked her, "Pavla, do you still love your mom a little? Just a little, so that you won't want to embitter her deeply?"

"I love her so much! As much as I loved her before! And maybe even more now," Pavla said animatedly and broke into a sob.

"Then, would you do her a favor? A secret one?"

"If it's going to make her happy, I will do it, no matter how difficult it may be!"

Natalia whispered the secret favor in her ear: a favor that filled her with surprise and outrage, but also with the desire to help her mother.

Arriving at the house, Pavla walked with fear into her mother's workshop. She was so sure that her father had had all the rooms of the house searched without finding any Christian materials, that she could not really believe there were so many books in that trunk. Now she and Natalia had to move everything to Natalia's house without their movements being noticed by the servants. To avoid suspicion, Pavla assigned them their chores over at the other end of the house and quietly opened the door to Natalia's servant, who came with his tools to unlock the trunk.

Her heart was beating fast from anxiety and worry. What if father came in suddenly? What if Helianos walked in? What kind of excuse would she find? Would they believe that she was doing it only for her mother's sake, and that she herself was not a Christian? Or would she pay dearly for her willingness to help?

But deep down, even in her anxiety, a sweet, soft joy was filling her. It was not a little thing to save this small fortune that her mother was keeping there and that she loved so much. It was not such a little thing to save it from disaster and to keep everything as a souvenir or a piece of memorabilia, even at the neighboring house. No one would ever find out about her contribution to this intrigue, since no one knew about the existence of the papers. Hand to hand, the papyrus scrolls and the books were transferred through the two little windows to the mansion across the way, from where they had originally come, without anyone suspecting it.

Natalia's servant, an old Christian, put the fabrics nicely together back into the trunk and put the locks on in a few minutes. The joy of his mistress was great after she realized that Adrian had not denied his faith, and it increased even more when she saw that their Christian books, with God's word, were safe and intact. Even in a house where so much hatred against the Christians prevailed, and while Tatiani was away!

Oh, if she only knew of the dangers in which they had been, and the different ways in which God had protected them! But such divine intervention is usually unknown to the poor mind of man, who is asked only for his warm glorification of God and his gratitude toward Him. Man's thanksgiving is enough in return for all His paternal intervention, without man's even noticing it, and maybe without his ever finding out about it!

Pavla held Ione on her knees and tried to feed her the last spoonfuls of her soup. And from the time the spoon came out of the silver bowl and reached Ione's mouth, she told her fables and chattered a thousand childish words. The white furry cat with its fluffy tail, which had been brought to them from the province of Cappadocia, was happy to be lying down at her mistress's feet, as more than a few times something good to eat dropped down from little Ione's hand.

Old Seviros, the grandfather, was submerged in his own miserable thoughts since he had heard the news from the prison, and he was occupying himself with trying to fix the handle of a carved censer, but without success.

There was nothing to show that anything had gone on before. And so Helianos was shocked when he came back home full of vengeance and opened the trunk. It was impossible! He couldn't believe his own eyes. He could not believe that his hands searched through the fabrics, throwing them everywhere around the room until the bottom of the trunk was visible, without finding even a single piece of parchment.

"The God of the Christians can read people's thoughts!" he said to himself in his shock.

There was no other explanation. He had not confided his angry thoughts to anyone. He had planned everything in secret. Who could have found out about it and prevented it? Who in their home knew the place where his mother had hidden the books so well? If it was someone from the household, why hadn't he or she hidden them or gotten rid of them before, in order to protect them all from the dangers in their home? Could it have been the servants? Impossible! Just yesterday he had been watching them all one by one, and had even started discussions with them in order to find out their beliefs. It was impossible that his siblings had had anything to do with it, since he knew them as well as he knew himself. Grandpa's advice to always respect the gods proved that he would not have protected the Christian books if he had found them.

He felt an undefined emotion inside. Awe. Fear. For the first time he felt himself small and weak. Could it be true that an invisible power was protecting the Christians? He also wished that one of the papyruses had been left behind so that he could keep it as a reminder. What a shame! His desire could not be fulfilled now! Who was responsible for this disappearance? When he suspected the little stained-glass window for a moment and opened it, there was nothing but the wall of the opposite building.

Natalia had well concealed the secret passage of the little window, leaving Urvinos' son to stew in his doubts. Then, with enormous care and protection, she had prepared the scrolls for Rufus to take with him. The news that had come from their holy Bishop made them all happy. Anthimos, the old Bishop of their Church, with his young heart and his many virtues, was one of the few Christians to come out alive from the torched church. Wanted by the Emperor's people, he was hiding far away from the city and was encouraging the faithful from there. The news that he was well and that he needed a few books for new converts not only pleased them deeply, but it gave many of the faithful the chance to escort the books so that they could be with him for a little while and receive his blessing. Rufus and another believer were chosen from among all the faithful for this very dangerous mission. They would leave that same night.

At the same time, at Urvinos' house the news about Helianos' own mission arrived. In a couple of days General Teaos would embark for Alexandria with his soldiers. Sent by the Emperor himself, he would inspect that great city and confirm whether or not the authorities were carrying out their duties according to the laws and the orders decreed by the Emperor.

Helianos received the order with great enthusiasm and immediately started preparing for the trip. At this moment he wanted nothing more than to leave Nicomedia, because it reminded him of the many terrible things that had happened. He wanted to go, even if he was unable to solve the mystery of the disappearing parchments.

9

MARTYRIC TROPHIES

WHENEVER Pavla met her friend Vassilla, all they talked about was the dresses that they saw being worn by the girls of their own age and the ladies of the nobility. The expensive fabrics that her father sold, some of which were embroidered with gold and silver thread, seemed more expensive and even prettier when worn by the wives and daughters of the senators and the generals; and especially so when they were elegantly combined with soft matching shawls placed gracefully across the shoulder, or with sheer, nearly transparent head veils. In the winter, lightweight furs of white, gray and tan, brought from Germany and scented with aromas from Palmyra, made the appearance of every lady even more majestic. And the precious stones that glittered on them spoke of their many riches. Indeed, this was their intention: to amaze the people around them with their wealth.

Vassilla and Pavla had once been exceedingly amused by a story they heard about a great Roman lady. She wore, so they said, a dress so thickly embroidered with emeralds and pearls that it had cost her an enormous forty million sestertii![1] In or-

1. The *sestertius* was a Roman-era silver coin worth about one-fourth of a denarius (which was about a day's pay for a physical laborer). Although difficult to quantify in terms of today's currency, forty million sestertii clearly represented a substantial sum of money.—ED.

der to convince everyone of its price and to have its value admired even more, whenever she wore the dress, the lady carried the sales receipt with her! The two friends had laughed hard when they heard this story. But deep inside they both admired these dresses and anyone else who could compete with this lady. And if the noble ladies of the kingdom could appear with so much luxury and wealth, they could only just imagine the indescribable brilliance of the Empress herself!

"Are you coming? I have heard that the Empress is going to be there, too." That was the message that Vassilla had brought to Pavla that day.

It was an unusual day, too. The Christians were deeply happy and so were the idolaters, and both for the same reason. The Count of the Imperial Guard, George, was to go to the temple of the idols, and the idolaters heard that he would offer sacrifices that day. What a great triumph for the Emperor, what a great victory for the Empire!

"Count George will offer sacrifices to Apollo!" the news coursed through the crowd of idolaters and filled them with enthusiasm and pride for their god's achievement.

George was not an average person. The whole city and country had been enthralled by the amazing events that had occurred and the astounding miracles that the great prisoner had performed. The Emperor and Galerius had not asked him to offer sacrifices to the gods when they first learned about his confession of faith. They had only asked him to recant it. How could they afford to lose such a brave man? But George would not compromise, and so the tortures had begun…. But whatever they had done to him, his wounds had healed instantly! They had thrown him in jail and placed a heavy rock on his chest, but all the while he prayed fervently to God, asking Him to keep his heart more steadfast and immovable than the rock itself. Then they had tied him to a wheel below which were fixed many sharp knives. Everyone believed that they would find George dead, cut to pieces. But when the Emperor and his entourage were on their way to the temple, thinking with satisfaction that they had finally finished him off, they suddenly saw George standing right in front of them!

It was not surprising then that, after this miracle, Anatolios* and Protoleon,* the generals, had taken off their swords and their military belts, placed them at the feet of the Emperor and declared that they too believed in Jesus Christ.

It was not a surprise either that many more officers had confessed their faith, while messengers informed the Emperor that many soldiers and civilians who were witnesses at the place of torture had confirmed that they too would become Christians. The Emperor's messengers added that they had made sure that none of them had remained alive.

George was subjected to new tortures. They threw him into a pit of lime up to his neck. Diocletian, refusing to believe that he would come out safely this time, went with his escorts to see for himself. When he saw George's face shining and healthy, he ordered them to take him out. George was as strong and as intact as ever!

"Who saved your life?" Diocletian asked him with surprise and shock.

"Even if I tell you, you still will not believe, so what's the point of unfruitful answers?" the martyr answered calmly.

"Still, I want to make it clear, O King, that Christ, the Son of God, is the One Who is protecting and guarding both me and all the faithful from every danger."

The following day they put his feet into red-hot iron shoes and made him run. They whipped him mercilessly. Again George remained unharmed by everything.

"If you want us to believe, perform a miracle!" said Magnentios, one of the bureaucrats, pointing to the dead body of a martyr that had been stacked along with others.

George knelt down and prayed fervently, and then said to the dead martyr, "In the name of Jesus Christ, rise and stand up!"

Immediately the dead martyr took life and arose! After that incident many people, civilians and soldiers alike, believed. The Emperor, furious and enraged, demanded that his high priest show the power of his magic and do the same. But through his prayers George neutralized all of the satanic energies of the wizard, so that the wizard himself also believed and cried out that he was a Christian, too!

How could the Emperor's decree prevent the crowds who daily visited George—all the people of Nicomedia who wanted to see this great martyr in person—from coming to his prison cell? Their throng was so great that the Emperor was forced to recall the decree out of fear that the people would revolt against him.

Who did not know about George, the Christian prisoner, the martyr, the victor? But what a shock it was to hear that their gods had defeated him, that George had become one of them! Could there be a greater triumph than to conquer such a champion? The idolaters, from the Emperor and the court functionaries to the simple people, were joyfully getting ready to go to the temple, where George would appear.

And the Christians were joyful because they were sure that new exploits of their faith, wrought by their great martyr brother, would win more souls and glorify the name of Christ.

"The Empress is going, too!" Pavla said happily upon hearing Vassilla's news. "We should leave very early so we can get good seats!"

Not only was it a great opportunity to see the Emperor and the Empress up close and to admire their majesty, but for Pavla it was also an unexpected help. What would her mother be able to say when she found out about the Christian officer's renunciation? How would she be able to refuse when Pavla begged her to imitate him? Then she would have so much to write about to Helianos, who was already so far away. His belief that it would be impossible for George to be indifferent about his great future, and that the Emperor would succeed in convincing him to remain loyal to him, had not been mistaken after all! Indeed, Pavla had so many things about which to write to her brother.

"Have you heard?" said someone in the crowd.

"Heard what?" replied another.

"The Empress is in prison!"

The shocking news that seemed like a dream, like a myth, was spreading from ear to ear like wildfire. Functionaries and beggars, masters and servants, wise elders and simple children were overcome with shock that left their eyes wide open and their minds stopped.

"In prison?" they would whisper and then fall silent, for they could not find anything else to say or to ask about such a unique and horrific event.

What had happened? How was it that the Empress, who had lived in the golden and marble-adorned palaces of that Diocletian whose ambition it was to surpass in glory the palaces of the Achaemedin, the Ptolemies and the Sassanidin,[1] all of a sudden found herself in the cold darkness of a prison?

"But why?" countless sets of lips whispered, seeking to learn more so as to assuage their doubts.

"Hmmm ... well ...," some of those who were better informed would hesitate to answer.

Would there be any consequences if someone divulged information like this, they wondered? *Should they keep the reason a secret?* They would struggle for a moment to hold their tongues, as if a chatterbox could really keep a secret, and then they would suddenly add with an air of confidentiality, "She said that she is a Christian!"

"A Christian?"

"The *Empress?!*"

"*Alexandra?*"*

The wife of Diocletian, the most implacable and cruelest persecutor of the Christians, was herself a Christian? Oh, thunderbolt! Oh, unexpected calamity!

"Oh, God of the Christians, are you so great, so strong, that you triumph so, even while you are being persecuted by all the powerful ones of this world? Are you so mighty that you put up your flag in the very heart of the camp of your

1. The Achaemedin of Persia, Ptolemies of Egypt and Sassanidin of Persia were famous imperial dynasties of the ancient world.—Ed.

enemies, so as to wrest your trophies from inside the very palace where decrees were signed ordering the eradication of the people bearing your name?" the lips of the people would whisper with awe.

The idolaters were amazed. The Christians were deeply moved. Everyone knew that Alexandra was not like Diocletian, with his harsh personality. She was quiet and simple, and the good works that she constantly performed, either in secret or with her courtiers, were well known to all the people. That was all anyone knew.

As for herself, all she had known about the Christians was that they were an unrespected people who were a danger to the security of the state. And now she was imprisoned for being a Christian! How was that possible? Had they made a mistake?

Like the rest, Pavla did not want to believe the rumor. But Vassilla, as a daughter of a high officer, had given her the right information.

Count George, who had touched so many souls with his patient endurance under extreme tortures, had not left Alexandra unmoved. While she was observing the cruel tortures they were inflicting on him, Alexandra had leaned over to the Emperor and begged him to stop them. Diocletian, thinking that she was not used to these kinds of spectacles, had told her to leave. But instead, she stood up and told him that such scenes were inhuman and unworthy of the crown. Was it the horror that she felt when Diocletian had blasphemed the name of Christ, or was it the faith that was beginning to form inside her? Whichever it was, full of a righteous inner strength, Alexandra announced that she too was a Christian!

When the Emperor tried to attribute her words to mental confusion, she had repeated her confession. And then the brutal order was heard: "The Empress shall be imprisoned!"

No one could save her from punishment and from the power of her husband's decrees, just as no one could save George. The Emperor was beyond the limits of his magnanimity. The anger of the crowds loyal to him demanded revenge. For not only had George not offered sacrifices in the temple of the idols, but with his prayers he had even compelled the demonic spirits living inside the idols to speak and to confess that Jesus Christ was the only true God that all people should worship!

George had to be executed.

He had shown contempt for them. He had put them all to shame. He had been victorious yet again. They had to punish him once and for all. They would have him beheaded. Diocletian pressed his lips tightly together, clenched his fists with the gold rings on his fingers, and with the look of a wild beast he added in a hoarse voice, "And let the Empress be beheaded, too!"

What else could come from out of the heart of the beast that was inside him?

Everyone felt horror upon hearing his decision. And some of them felt an infinite respect for her, who disregarded the crown and the purple mantle of glory and even her life itself for the sake of her new faith. What strength did this faith of the Christians hold? What was this attraction that so captivated their souls? Should they too learn about it and find out about its Treasures, which nullified all the other treasures of the world?

Apollos* made the decision right then and there. So did Isaakios* and Kodratos.* All three of them had been courtiers and members of the Empress's entourage, and her example made them think and worry. Should they put away all their prejudice and find out more about this persecuted Christian religion?

Putting aside their biases, they visited the house of a Christian priest and all three of them came out believers. So what if they knew that Diocletian's anger was waiting for them? They now knew about the Treasures. They did not hesitate to confess their faith, and they also did not hesitate to criticize the Emperor for his cruelty towards the Empress. And as they did not hesitate, they soon faced martyrdom.

Nor were they the only courtiers who became Christians. Theonas,* Christopher,* Antoninos* and Kesarios,* all members of the Emperor's entourage who had witnessed George's martyrdom, were shaken. They too thought that this faith that gave so much strength to its followers should become theirs. And so it did. And along with so many other government officials and simple people in those days, they courageously signed their confessions with their own blood.

Upon hearing the information Vassilla had to tell her, Pavla fell deep into thought. These were no small events. These were not average people who followed her mother's faith. And now was she supposed to go back to the prison and ask her to renounce it? She was sure that her mother already knew about the Empress, about the Count and the other courtiers. She would be overjoyed, Pavla was certain. And her mother's resolve not to recant and deny her faith would be even stronger. And so …

"So, my mother will be martyred soon," she said sadly. "I'm losing every hope!"

"*You are losing?*" said a voice from somewhere. "*On the contrary, you are finding! You are finding many hopes, infinite hopes! So many that this world cannot hold them. Don't you see how many people are abandoning everything for these hopes?*"

"Who said that?" Pavla said, frightened that words like these were heard for the first time ever in their house.

"I don't know," Vassilla whispered, "but whoever said it, she is right!"

10

THE FIRST RAYS

Turning-belt: it wasn't a very easy game.

The way they wrapped the double strap with the many complicated twists and knots over and over again, anyone would say that it could never be untied. And it was even more unimaginable for the middle to appear before the belt was actually unwrapped. But there were those who would place a sharp needle at the point they believed to be the center, and they would not miss. They were the winners, and much applause and cheers could be heard throughout the banquet halls. And often the cheers were accompanied by gifts and expensive awards.

At this time a winner had not yet appeared. No one attending the banquet, given by Arrianos the Eparch on the large veranda of his villa, could manage to put the needle in the right spot, and so the game would start all over again from the beginning.

General Teaos had tried twice without success, and the Eparch had driven the needle in more at the end than at the center of the belt, making everyone laugh hard. In the same way, the rest of the officers had missed the mark.

Helianos, as the General's protégé, had also been invited to the luncheon, and was watching the game from his seat, without thinking that he could participate. But Teaos did not forget him.

"Should my protégé try?" he asked the Eparch, thinking that Helianos' better sight might make a difference.

"Of course, he should play! Come on, young man! And if you win, my gold cup is yours!" he said generously.

Helianos blushed all the way to the roots of his hair. His new military uniform suited his tall, strong figure, and the General felt proud of his choice as he saw him standing out among the rest. Helianos took the needle and carefully observed the belt, especially the complicated wrapping with the knots and the turns, and then he steadily drove the needle in at a certain point.

The servant untied the strap and folded it in two, and the needle was found to be stuck right in the center of the target. The winner was revealed!

The applause and cheers were boisterous on the veranda, making the parrot, tied there by his shiny chain to the branch of a lotus tree, flutter with fear. The golden cup of the Eparch changed owners according to his promise. Helianos would have the best souvenir, along with the most entertaining impressions of his first trip to Egypt.

Finally, various fruits, sweet dates and reddish honey-glazed lotus buds were offered on water-lily leaves placed on large silver platters. The land of the Nile with its exotic beauty had a thousand new things to offer and with which to welcome each and every visitor. There were many different wild animals and plants, unique and unknown to other countries. Helianos made known to the General his desire to go further south along the banks of the Nile and to see up close the full groves of papyrus trees and the tall reeds where herons and crocodiles were hiding. He wanted to see with his own eyes the banks of the river becoming so narrow that he could touch them with his oars and then so wide again that it would remind him of a second ocean. He wanted to experience all of the paradoxes that he had only heard about as fairy tales from his well-traveled grandfather.

"The only person he won't see is Paphnutios!"* Arrianos said, breaking out in laughter, when Teaos repeated aloud his protégé's desire.

Seeing everyone's faces frowning from doubt, he hurried to give an explanation of what he had just said:

"He is one of these dangerous Christians who influences everybody. I was trying to figure out a way to arrest him, when one day, as I was getting off a boat onto one of the banks of the Nile, I saw somebody coming toward me.

" 'I heard you were looking for me,' he said, 'and I didn't want to put you to any trouble. I am Paphnutios.' I tried with all conscientiousness to keep the Emperor's decrees and ordered him tortured vigorously. The result was that his wounds closed and were healed, and the soldiers who were torturing him became Christians along with another forty* notables who were in jail with him and, I guess, listened to his words! But all of them paid for it dearly. Two of them lost their heads and the rest experienced how well the Eparch's fire burns! But the main perpetrator disappeared. I believe, my General, that your protégé won't meet him again around the Nile! That is, unless he deeply desires to carry out the orders of the divine Emperor and Paphnutios appears again in front of him, like he did to me!"

Arrianos laughed, glad that Teaos was listening to his exploits and would convey them to their lord. He was not like

Prokopios,* for example, whom Diocletian had appointed Eparch of Alexandria, giving him orders to persecute the Christians. Instead of obeying the Emperor's command, Prokopios had not only supported the Christians but was rumored to have become one of them. It was a good thing that he had resigned and left Alexandria, because he would have defamed the title of Eparch with such behavior. Arrianos would never be like him.

The luncheon was about to end and all the participants were about to leave, when a new angry case arrived at the Eparch's house.

"The sons of the men you burned, Eparch, are committing the same crime their fathers did!" a military man yelled angrily from the garden door.

"Are they many?" Arrianos asked with anger. "Did they say that they were Christians?"

"Sixteen! Sixteen boys. They're like kids! They're not afraid of talking openly about Christianity!"

Arrianos could not have manufactured a better opportunity to show his blind obedience to the Emperor's decrees and their strict enforcement.

He ordered the children to come to one of their temples and asked Teaos, by his presence, to help him carry out this great responsibility and make sure that the people would obey the laws of the State. Helianos followed them, but his mind was still on the game he had just won and on the praises he had received. Once he was standing in front of the sixteen young men, however, he looked at them with surprise.

Their heads were lifted up, their foreheads shining and

their eyes sparkling! They reminded him of Rhodon and the rest of the students of the Babylas School whom he had met on his way that day several weeks before. Were the Christians all so alike, even though they lived in different parts of the world? They reminded him of his mother—his mother whom he had not even wanted to hug good-bye—with her unbending behavior. Were the Christians all so alike, no matter what their age?

How old could these boys be? Most of them were around his own age. Some were a little older and others were a little younger, like the last one on the end with the big eyes and the red cheeks, who couldn't have been more than thirteen. He was the same age and height as Helianos' brother, Antiochos.

Arrianos rolled out the parchments with the decrees of the persecution and tried to convince them to change their minds, explaining to them the consequences that their refusal would bring. First he turned to the youngest.

Then something unexpected happened.

With eyes like an eagle's, his cheeks and lips red like fire, the boy asked to see the infamous parchment.

"Good for you! Read it and you'll be saved!" the Eparch said with enthusiasm, certain about his first conquest.

His enthusiasm chilled suddenly. His face became pale. His eyes darkened with horror and rage. The child took the parchment in his hands with an unexpected boldness that seemed like it belonged to a brave general entering unrestrained onto the battlefield, ran to the nearest altar, and threw it into the fire that was burning. At the same time, like a triumphant war cry, like a cry of joy, he said victoriously, "One is God! The Father of our Lord Jesus Christ!"

"Bravo, brave little eagle!" a cheer escaped from Helianos' lips, but was drowned out by the wild and angry hub-bub of the crowd.

The idol-worshipping temple sorcerers became mad with anger. A child of thirteen had put them to shame with his indescribable courage. The Eparch went berserk. He rushed toward the little Christian, grabbed him in a frenzy, and with his own hands threw him onto the burning altar.

In seconds the boy's soft skin started burning, while his big eyes and beautiful face kept shining through the flames with a divine joy. He looked at his fifteen friends, who, full of sacred desire and enthusiasm, were pleading with him to pray that they too might wear the martyr's wreath, as their fathers and he had done before them.

"See you all up there!" he seemed to say, and smiled.

Then he lifted up his half-burnt hand and the young martyr made the sign of the Cross on his face. His strength was leaving him. His life was ebbing away. This fresh flower was closing its petals before it even had a chance to open them all the way; but it was closing them now in order to be able to open them again, refreshed, unfading and eternal, in the garden of everlasting heavenly joy....

Then he leaned his head on the coals of the fire and let his last look fall on Helianos. And his gaze stayed fixed there, until the fire went out in ashes and smoke....

With his eyes full of tears, Helianos stared with shock. He held the young martyr's last look inside himself with a sacred passion, indelible in the depths of his memory and heart. He felt like running toward him, putting his arms into the fire to hug and kiss him, and asking him secretly: *Tell me ... tell me ... what secrets does this faith of yours hold that you love it so much? Tell me, so I can love it too!*

He saw Teaos pale, looking at him. Then he came to his senses. The bitter, ironic tightness around the General's lips showed his disgust—what he felt about the sorry state of the Empire and for its glorious power, which could execute dangerous enemies—thirteen-year-old children!

The General was ready to go and Helianos followed him painfully. Was it that his knees could no longer move well, or was it the sympathy that was born inside him for those fifteen young men condemned to death, who were standing right there in front of him, brave and intrepid? They stood there in the full vigor of their youth, optimistic as princes awaiting a royal inheritance, erect and with brilliant foreheads, like victors waiting to wear a precious Purple Mantle around their shoulders. He wanted to tell them how much he admired them—that he was jealous of them, that he could distinguish in them, condemned to death as they were, something great and superhuman! Should he ask the General or the Eparch to let them free and allow them to live? Or would he take something great away from them by doing so?

He looked at them again with love and respect, and bent his head when he saw that they were looking at him. He followed the General quietly, with a new world of sensibilities and feelings inside himself—a new world that was based on the first humble thought of his life: that many young men of his age were surpassing him in merit and in strength!

Later that night he found out that the fifteen friends of the brave little eagle had been taken outside the city and had all accepted a martyr's death by the executioner's lance, with the same courage and bravery. They even accepted it chanting hymns!

"Please let's never be present at another Christian's torturous martyrdom," he said to the General as they were walking by the same street on which the temple was located, understanding that he was thinking the same thing.

Now that he heard about the execution of the fifteen young men, he felt the desire to be near them, to look straight into their eyes that reflected such clear horizons, to hear their voices, their words, their chanting....

That night he dreamt that he had run and found them, there outside of the city, that he bent over their bodies covered with blood from the lance-wounds, and that he begged them fervently, "Tell me.... Tell me what is hidden behind your faith that you love it so much? Tell me so I can love it too ... so I can run to my mother, to make up for my bad behavior...."

When he woke up in the morning, he realized his pillow was wet with tears.

His fear that he would never see his mother again had given way to his excitement about the permission that the Emperor had given for his trip. But now his guilt about his bad behavior would often come to shake him, to fill him with repentance, even in his sleep. He was never more homesick for Nicomedia than he was that morning, feeling the necessity of going back to make up and beg for his mother's forgiveness.

But the journey back home would take time.

The time passed by quickly as Teaos inspected the various eparchies in Egypt, and soon he was close to finishing his duties in the various political and military administrations. They went everywhere around the land of the Nile. They visited the enigmatic Sphinx and the Pharaohs' pyramids. Helianos looked at everything with insatiable eyes. He bought souvenirs, fabrics, local crafts and jewelry for his family and his relatives. He collected unique flowers and leaves and dried them by placing them between two pieces of papyrus pressed under the weight of a heavy piece of carved cedarwood, and when he had free time he enjoyed spending hours reading at the famous and fabulously rich library in Alexandria. The only thing he could not find on its shelves were Christian papyruses. He wondered whether the persecutions had destroyed them, or whether some other invisible Christian hands had protected them, like the ones in his mother's workshop. How he wished to meet someone so that he could learn more about this new religion of martyrs and heroes!

One day, as he was looking for a blue flower in the bushes and cane stalks by the bank of the Nile, he saw something white that captured his attention. It was a small, tightly wrapped book. Without knowing what it was, he picked it up and hid it in the case of his lance. But their Egyptian driver saw him.

"Are you a brother?" he leaned forward and asked him in a low voice.

Helianos did not want to give any explanations, but he also did not want to say no.

"How did this get here?" he asked in a quiet voice.

"This is the place where Paphnutios* preached the gospel to those eighty fishermen. Somebody probably hid it before being arrested and tortured."

"Why? Did they believe instantly and then become martyrs?"

"All eighty of them! And later the Councilor Eusebios and four-hundred soldiers who were present at his martyrdom believed! Not many days ago they threw all of them into four huge furnaces. But you are a stranger and obviously you haven't heard about it yet."

"So Paphnutios went and presented himself to Arrianos again?"

"Of course! When Arrianos threw him into the sea with a huge rock tied around his neck, the saint came up to the surface and spoke to him about our Christ's power. The Eparch didn't know what else to do…. He arrested him again and sent him, they said, to the Emperor with a report of all the wonders that he performed. This is how Christ blesses His saints!"

A soldier came close and they both stopped their conversation.

As long as the General's assigned journey kept them in the riverboats at night, it was not easy for Helianos to find a corner or a spot of his own, away from the looks of the rest of the soldiers. But when they went back to Alexandria, to the private house which was close to the military headquarters, and which was available for the officials and dignitaries, there was a small room next to the General's that was at his disposal.

That was the only place where he could take out the papyrus from the depth of his lance case. With a pair of tweezers he cleaned the wicks of the four-flame lamp and then carefully rolled out the papyrus next to the lamp. He started reading with respect and thirst, with the desire to learn, with a clear mind. It was a part of Christ's teaching that was talking about love—about the love that His followers should have among themselves, and the love they would show to Him by their obedience to His commandments. And it finished with a little prayer for them:

"I am not asking You to take them from this world, but to keep them away from the evil one.... Sanctify them in Your truth; Your word is the truth ... and the glory You gave Me, I have given it to them...."

Helianos recalled the Egyptian guide. One night when the soldiers invited the guide to keep them company and he realized that their discussions were unsavory, he found an excuse to leave right away. Hadn't Rhodon always done the same? The Christians seemed to have this desire and struggle to "keep away from the evil one": with the help of their God to stay away from bad and evil—and there was certainly a lot of evil prevailing in those days—and to live a life of light wherever they were. Is this what the word "saint" meant when the Egyptian guide referred to it? What else did "sanctify them in Your truth" mean?

Bending over the lamp, Helianos was trying to explain to himself these words he was reading, when the door suddenly opened and made him jump away. With one move he tried to hide the papyrus but it rolled down on the floor.

"I got a letter from Nicomedia!" the General said, upset. "Did they write something to you, too?"

"No! I didn't get one yet," Helianos answered.

Before, he would have said that this papyrus was from home. He would have made up a story to escape from danger if somebody had asked him what he was reading. But he didn't lie. And he felt it was so good to be "kept away from evil."

"I can't get this through my head! I just can't believe it,

although it's my wife who is writing this letter!" Teaos continued. "She writes it clearly: The Empress Alexandra became a Christian and died...."

"The Empress a Christian?"

"A Christian woman taught her about Christianity, but what finally did it was that she believed in George's martyrdom...."

"The Count martyred?"

"They say that he went through a lot of tortures, but each time he would come out without a scratch, and that he performed many miracles. In the end they beheaded him. The Emperor ordered the Empress to be beheaded, too, but they didn't get to carry out his command. They found her dead in the jail cell they put her in!"[1]

Two tears shone on the red cheeks of the young attaché, as the four flames of the lamp danced beside him. His prediction about the young officer of the Imperial Guard had been very wrong. Were his tears because of his mistake, or were they because of his desire to be close to his hero, to ask him about the secret that made him deny his earthly glory? Or were they for the brave queen and her sacrifice?

"The glory You gave me, I have given to them ...": the words he had read came into his mind like a flash of lightning. They had denied their glory, yes. But was it not glory, this admiration that he (and who knew how many others?) felt for them because of their very self-denial? Was it not glory that they could "keep away from the evil one" and be

---

1. Although Alexandra* wished to accept tortures for the sake of her faith in Christ, she prayed to God to take her soul so that her death would not burden Diocletian with greater sins. Her prayer was heard. She died two days before the decapitation of Saint George.—AUTH.

"sanctified in His truth"? This must be the glory that his mother had spoken to him about that evening, when she said to him, "And you should think seriously, when you desire the glory that the Purple Mantle gives, about the glory that virtue gives, the glory that goodness gives...." This must be the glory that she meant, when in prison she had told them about the grand future that continues unendingly, even after life on this earth.

"Are you crying, Helianos?" Teaos said, rousing him out of his thoughts. "I cried, too! What's going to happen to the Empire, which is losing all these great figures? I didn't tell you, but many courtiers and military officers were killed for the same reason."

"Others will take their places, General!" Helianos answered brightly.

"Yes, others will replace them, but they won't be the same!"

"If they have the same beliefs, they will!"

"Where did you get such a weird thought?... But maybe you're right! We should learn more about this religion that we are persecuting so harshly. Maybe their Christian beliefs make them different from the rest of us."

Helianos was deeply overjoyed when he realized that his protector, whom he admired and appreciated so much, shared his own ideas and questions. But they didn't have a chance to say any more.

"And now I should announce to you another message from Nicomedia," the General continued. "We have been ordered, on our way back home, to go first by way of your forefathers' land."

"Through Thessalonica?" Helianos cried out joyfully.

"Exactly. During that time the Emperor might be there. Besides the military matters that we are going to discuss, our mission will be to attribute honors to him. We are leaving in ten days!"

It took a long while for him to go to sleep that night. Which news kept his mind awake? Was it the news about the martyred Count? As clear as the Emperor's promise had been, it did not lessen his anxiety about his mother's imprisonment. Helianos went to sleep very late that night.

11

THE SAINTS WERE LIKE US

THE two white horses galloped along the country road. As they went further away from the city, the vegetable gardens, the orchards and the vineyards with their ripe bunches of grapes disappeared and gave way to fields of sheep and forested hills.

No one in the spacious carriage paid attention to the scenic view as it changed from time to time. The wide, comfortable, light gray pillows with the yellow cords around them did not relax any of the passengers as they had done on other trips, nor was the long low stool with the yellow tassels used for its intended purpose of supporting their feet. Pavla and Vassilla, having left their seats, were sitting on one side of the stool and listening ecstatically to what Aroe was saying. They wanted to have her right across from them so that they could look straight at her and not miss a word.

Vassilla had never imagined that there was a Christian family among her relatives. On that recent day when Pavla had been talking about her lost hopes and had received an unexpected answer, they had seen Aroe, the daughter of Diogenis, Nicomedia's greatest landowner and Vassilla's uncle. In the youthful enthusiasm of her seventeen years, Aroe could not hold back her joy at the news that in the midst of the persecution their faith had won an Empress, and she spoke openly to them without hesitating. Their hearts had accepted her words like fresh drops of dew, and since that time the three friends had sought every chance to meet so that they could talk about more important and interesting matters than the dresses and the jewelry of the ladies of the aristocracy.

Now that Aroe was going to her farm, Vassilla and Pavla got permission from their families to spend a day with her in the country. It was not the beauty of the countryside that attracted them so, nor was it the ride in the comfortable carriage. Neither was it the chance that the three of them had when they were alone together to talk about their faith without being afraid that someone would overhear them. Rather, this was an altogether exceptional opportunity, which they anticipated eagerly.

At the end of the property, hidden behind a line of trees, was Diogenis' farmhouse. No one even noticed its existence unless they paid careful attention. It was not very difficult for the Christians from the city and the neighboring towns to gather there in order to worship God and celebrate the Divine Liturgy, and to hear His word through the sermon. These meetings in the countryside—with the peace that they brought, and the communion between all the brothers and sisters—became a source of energy and a provision of joy, a place of strengthening for the difficult times they were all going through.

There they chanted hymns, and they partook of the Holy Gifts, the Sacred Body and Precious Blood of their Lord, the food of life and strength. They would honor the heroic athletes of their faith, the martyrs, keeping their holy relics in precious cases and writing about their torture, their martyrdom and their God-inspired defense of the faith. They would also celebrate and welcome those who were new to the faith, who appeared at the church desiring to be baptized, defying the dangers that threatened their future. Moreover, the generous offerings that were gathered without end—offerings of pure love with their pious and silent voices—showed forth the warm hearts of the brothers and sisters and filled them all with enthusiasm for the sake of the elect who surrounded them.

Each of them was experiencing something of the blessed olden times of the first Church, where the multitude of the faithful were one in heart and soul. Even in normal times the Christians of the area would feel deeply joyful at the thought of such a meeting, but this time they waited for it with a special eagerness. They had been informed that there was a possibility that their Bishop, Anthimos, would join them. They all felt an inseparable bond with him. It was true that the Emperor's soldiers were trying to find his whereabouts so that they could hurt the Church of Nicomedia through its hierarchy. Perhaps, they thought, if he who was always the first one to support the Christians was not there to motivate them with his kindness, his gentle influence and his passionate words, then they would not persist in their beliefs. If they eliminated the general, they would conquer his army, they thought. But their search was fruitless.

Aroe had waited anxiously for this day, and she had transmitted her enthusiasm to her girlfriends. It was no small thing for each of them to receive his personal blessing, especially for Pavla who wanted to ask for his prayers on behalf of her prisoner-mother, who was humbly sending her respects through her daughter. But at that moment in the carriage, the discussion that had captivated their attention was different....

Kyriaki* was not a stranger to them. Vassilla had met her once when she had gone to visit Melitini, her mother's native land, and she had admired Kyriaki's beauty so much that upon her return to Nicomedia she had brought up a discussion about her with her friends. Now Aroe had other news to tell them. Some days before, Kyriaki, in the blossom of her youth and beauty—the same age as they were—had offered herself as a sacrifice for her faith!

The Eparch of Bythinia had managed to convert some unstable Christians to pagan idolatry, and his co-Eparch colleagues from Melitini and Nicomedia thought of sending Kyriaki to him, in the belief that his methods of persuasion would win her over, as well.

"I can just imagine her! She wouldn't have been scared at all!" Vassilla said with passion.

"Been scared?" replied Aroe enthusiastically. "She spoke a lot more convincingly than he did when he told her to feel sorry for her beauty and youth. 'I learned the value of physical beauty well from the wrinkles that are awaiting it and from the grave that is calling it,' she answered steadily. 'You called me "rose," Eparch! But haven't you ever seen the meaning of the life of a rose? I don't know of anything sadder than the temporary blooming and appearing of a rose that is so quickly annihilated by decay.'"

"Oh! She said it really well!" Pavla interrupted in her excitement.

"And then she continued with amazing courage: 'Did you ever think for a moment that I as a Christian would do such a foolish thing as to lose eternal glory in order to stay a little while longer on this earth? I gave you my answer before, Eparch, and I am repeating it to you again: I am and I will be a Christian both in life and in death!' "

"What a great declaration! 'I am and I will be a Christian in life and in death,'" Vassilla repeated with awe.

"And I fought so hard to try to convince my mother to … not to be a Christian in death!" Pavla whispered regretfully.

"When people are not aware of the truth, God forgives their ignorance," Aroe said tenderly. "When they know, then they declare it, like Kyriaki."

"I am and will be, in life and in death, a Christian!"

"What joy contained in just twelve words!…"

None of them spoke for a while. They wanted to think over and over again about those twelve words, so that they too could experience a foretaste of their joy.

"Did they torture her badly?" Vassilla asked, first to break the silence.

"Brutally and mercilessly. But the next day Kyriaki was as strong as the day before. The Eparch was speechless! 'Do you want to see, Eparch, that with the power of my Christ I am stronger than your gods?' the martyr said. 'Here are your temples. If you want, let's go there where I can prove it to you. And if I cannot, then you'll be the winner!' The Eparch, although hesitant at first, accepted. And even though there were many officials gathered in the temple, after Kyriaki's prayer an earthquake shook the whole place. The idols fell down in pieces and some of them fell on the Eparch and killed him!"

"I'm sure a lot of the people present became believers after such a great miracle," Pavla said.

"Oh yes, of course! Many believed. The rest were scattered and Kyriaki was free to preach about Christ's truth. When the new Eparch was appointed, he arrested her again and threw her first into fire and then to a hungry lion. But neither the fire nor the lion touched her. In the end he ordered to have her beheaded, but just as the executioner was about to perform the act, Kyriaki asked to pray. There, on the very spot of her execution, she passed away peacefully, to receive the wreath of glory from the hand of our Lord!"

"May she intercede in prayer for us in her glory," Vassilla whispered with respect. Her mind went back to Kyriaki, as she first met her at that house in Melitini. She was so young! A girl, just like them! What kind of power did her faith give her, that she could shatter idols and overcome executions and tortures? How much joy did her faith fill her with?

"A girl like us became a saint!" she whispered thoughtfully. "Can you imagine?"

"All the saints were and are just like us!" Aroe said. "But they love our faith deeply. And this love becomes virtue in times of peace and in times of persecution—virtue and sacrifice! It is our choice whether to imitate them or not!"

The two white horses stopped their galloping and turned into a narrow alley. An opening in the bushes, very difficult to distinguish but well known to them, led them into Diogenis' farmhouse from the backyard. Visitors reached Diogenis' house from many different hidden alleys and pathways around the area, so that they would have no fear of raising the suspicion of some traveler on the main road.

Everything was quiet when they arrived. The big black and white farm dog welcomed Aroe with great leaps and the wagging of its tail, but without barking. It had been trained not to show that anyone was approaching its master's house at this time. Vassilla and Pavla looked around with admiration at the long lines of fruit trees, the pigeons' nests, the beehives, and the flower beds surrounding the simple but well built house.

Quiet, melodious chanting enveloped them with tender feeling as they found themselves in the spacious covered yard, which was enclosed all around with galleries and rooms so that no sounds would spill out into the back or front yards. It was the first time that the girls had heard hymns chanted by so many of the faithful together, and it seemed to them that this small corner was a part of heaven, full of angelic harmony.

As they entered the room where all the faithful were gathered, a parchment over the door, beautifully written by the hand of a calligrapher, seized their attention. It read: "He makes them new in His love and rejoices with them in enjoyment as in a day of celebration." They were the words of a prophet. So what if they did not know how to interpret them? They saw the words written in the shiny faces, the clear happy eyes, and the brotherly cordiality that was overflowing all around. It was a new, different, and beautiful world within the world in which they were living! In his or her own love, each one of them renewed their Lord's love and rejoiced with Him as in a great everlasting celebration!

"Look at our new books!" Aroe said joyfully, showing them a bunch of new books sitting on the shelves, wrapped around with thin red ribbons. They had been written a little while before the persecutions were ordered, and now they were being given to newly enlightened brothers and sisters. Who knew what brotherly hands had protected them up until now so that they would be safe?

Pavla blushed.

What hands? M … m … mine! The answer came up to her lips. But she kept it inside. No, she wouldn't allow pride and boastfulness to show, as before. In this new beautiful world, she should strive to be new also.

"May God reward those who wrote them so that our souls may be fed," she said humbly and gratefully.

She remembered the words of the parchment. "He makes them new in His love." She felt in her heart the renovating power of His love and rejoiced deeply with inexpressible joy. She also felt something of the joyful, permanent celebration! How much happier everyone would be if they could manage these triumphs of virtue more often!

It was late in the afternoon when they appeared around the turn. Tired, sweaty, they hastened to show their exasperation to the traveler they had just stopped. Did he know where the Bishop of the Christians was hiding during all this time, when the Emperor had a warrant out for his arrest? Even in their detailed investigations and searches they had not managed to find him.

"Do you know where he is hiding, old man?"

The old man placed his serene sight on them. How tired these poor soldiers looked! His face shone in an instant.

"My children, you are very tired and hungry," he said calmly. "I do know Anthimos and I also know where he lives. I will show him to you, after you accept a little food and rest a while. Would you like to come to my humble home?"

The officer and the soldiers accepted the invitation and the unexpected hospitality with pleasure. When they had eaten and rested, they asked him to help them with their mission. Then they heard the shocking answer, "I am Anthimos!"

His serene face, his sweet smile, the fearless look made them admit that they were facing a hero. Should they touch him? Should they cuff him in chains and drag him to the examining magistrate? It seemed to them a kind of desecration. It also seemed to them a kind of nakedness of every trace of humanity within themselves. No, they would not arrest him.

They told him to leave, to go far away. They would return to their superiors and assure them that all their searches had been in vain—that they had not found him anywhere.

But then the hero became even more heroic. Support his salvation upon a lie? Never!

"No, you will take me," he ordered them firmly. "And if you won't turn me in, I will turn myself in!"

This religion is full of great people and we are persecuting them! their silent, ecstatic, tearful eyes seemed to say.

Nothing else could be done. Anthimos would be presented to the Emperor in Nicomedia for martyrdom, like so many of his spiritual children in the city covered with blood....

At Diogenis' house, the faithful did not see their Bishop that day. Vassilla and Pavla never met him. They held some of his words that had been conveyed by the priest deeply in their hearts, and made a secret promise to keep them with all their might. Virtue and steadfastness would be their great and most cherished aim. Virtue and steadfastness: that was his eternal advice.

12

DEATH TO THE WINNER

THE words echoed inside him like a reveille trumpet. In a moment the huge racecourse with the colorful crowd faded from in front of his eyes. The court functionaries with their official uniforms, the soldiers with their naked swords, and the various athletes with their green and gray short tunics vanished from his sight. The tripods with the fragrant incense and the flower wreaths around the arena, the officers of the Imperial Guard and the Emperor himself, in his gold-adorned spectator's box, with his majestic purple mantle and his pearl diadem, were no longer noticed by the thin young man who stood in the audience next to Helianos.

Only one thing remained:

A giant-figured, infamous athlete who was incomparable in skill and strength, and who had no competitors. Who would dare fight against the incredible Lyaeos, who always won, wiping out all his rivals? The sight of him alone was enough to banish the will to fight of even the most famous athletes. As a result, no one came forward in answer to the repeated challenges of the announcer.

But this last invitation also had an unexpected addition:

"Which one of the Christians," he said, "has the courage, believing in his God, to fight Lyaeos, who is under the protection of the gods? Who? Let him come forward!"

"Which one of the Christians?..."

The announcer stopped for a second. His words were still echoing vividly like a reveille trumpet.

The thin young man next to Helianos stood there staring straight ahead, without seeing any of the big hippodrome in Thessalonica, where races were organized in honor of Diocletian. He could only see Lyaeos standing across the stadium, robust, proud and all-powerful—Lyaeos and his false, nonexistent gods on one side.

But on the other side? The almighty power of his God! His eyes sparkled. From what world and what heaven did this spark come down that made his thin face even brighter? What thought brought on this spark? No, he had never thought of hurting anyone. He had never even had a small fight or a scratch. But the announcer's challenge turned him inside out. The enemies seemed to triumph with this challenge. Lyaeos' power strengthened the disbelief of the people and encouraged the boast of idolatry. Should he just sit there and let them triumph?

No, he had to do something. His thin hand, the most inexperienced in this kind of fight, would be held by an angel's hand that would crush the enemy. The enemy of his faith, the enemy of the life of the souls of so many people! Of course, such an intervention would cost him his life. The Emperor and the people would probably not recognize such a victory and would punish him. After all, was he sure that this was the right thing to do? Should he not ask for someone's opinion or for someone's support and prayers?

A sweet face, respected and beloved, came to his mind. His good friend, his wise teacher who was teaching him the catechism of the faith! So what if he too was young, only a few years older than he was? Demetrios* was a great influence on him, not because of his high honors or his imposing appearance nor even because of his charming eloquence, but because of his grace and his virtue.

Many young people from Thessalonica would gather around Demetrios in the underground rooms of the Chalceuphtic Arcade and would listen to him talking to them about Christ and explaining passages from the Holy Scriptures. Those evenings and dawns—the only quiet hours, since their shelter was near the public baths—offered them the beauty of a new sunrise in their souls. Many young people became Christians because of his words and his example. Among them was Nestor.*

When Demetrios was arrested and put in prison after his brave declaration in front of the Emperor ("I believe only in my Christ!" he had proclaimed), Nestor had managed to visit him at the jail. The bonds of a spiritual friendship are never shattered by the bonds of prison! And at this moment he needed this friendship more than anything. He quickly thrust aside Helianos, who was standing next to him, and ran out of the stadium.

Where is this young guy suddenly going so fast? Helianos wondered, readjusting his robe that had been dislodged by Nestor's quick passage.

Tired from the journey, Helianos was watching the races distractedly. The rough voyage by ship, during which time they had been buffeted by huge waves in the middle of the sea and had faced death at almost every moment, had made them realize how unable their gods were to support them in those difficult hours. They saw how incapable their gods were of giving them something of the inner peace that the faith of their ship's captain, Pouplios, gave him. Everyone had envied his trust in his God and his love for Him, as well as his strength and his physical resistance in that danger. To be sure, no one had thought of applying the Emperor's decree against him for being a Christian.

They had docked afterward on a deserted island, waiting for a few days for the strong head wind to stop, so they had not been able to get to Thessalonica earlier than the evening of the day before. All Helianos' plans to go and meet his relatives were in vain. All the dreams he had had during the journey, of walking around the big beautiful city street by street, reliving his grandfather's narration, were limited for the time being to the admiration he felt while looking at the triumphant Apse of Galerius. Galerius had built it there a few years before, when he had fought a war against the Persians and won, so as to remind the people of the city, together with the visitors who walked along the Egnatian Way, of his great achievement.

The whole building consisted of two huge triple arches[1] in parallel lines, in the midst of which arose a half dome standing in four high arches that formed a square. Finely made embossed figures, carved on the white stone of the thick base of the lower arches and divided into four zones with garlands made of branches and flowers, depicted Caesar's triumphant campaign. On another part, some conquered Easterners were kneeling in front of him begging for his mercy. Somewhere else, the locals of the city were welcoming him at the gates. Elsewhere he was depicted talking to his soldiers, who surrounded him with raised banners,

---

1. One of these two triple arches is preserved up to the present day.—Auth.

and further up he was shown offering sacrifices along with Emperor Diocletian in front of an altar, in thanksgiving for his victories.

With great interest, Helianos scrutinized the arch that was close to the stadium. The land of Macedonia always brought to his mind the glorified King Philip; and, even more, the brave young man who had left from Pella one day with thirty thousand infantry and four thousand five hundred riders to fight the barbarians and bring Hellenic[1] civilization from Mysia and Bythinia to Babylon, Persia, Libya and even the rivers of India.

From his early years, Helianos' hero had been Alexander the Great, whose conquests attracted him and stirred his ambitions. *A bigger, incomparably bigger, arch should be built for him,* he thought, although he believed that the greatest achievements always stayed in people's memories, even when there were no buildings to remind them. But even the kind of glory given to Galerius was not too small to wish for himself. With these thoughts absorbing his mind, he was carelessly watching the progress of the games in the racecourse when a sudden unrest resounded around the stadium.

"This skinny guy?" someone asked.

"This young boy?" repeated another.

"Who is he? He's never appeared in the stadium before. He's never taken part in the games."

"Ha! Ha! He's gonna fight the unbeatable Lyaeos? It's obvious he doesn't know what the amphitheater is all about. Tell him to have a little pity for his youth!"

The spectators, with their bodies bent forward and their

---

1. *Hellenic* refers to the civilization and culture of the Greeks, dating back to ancient times.—ED.

necks craned, stared amazed and commented sarcastically on the young man who had appeared in the arena to compete against the frightful Lyaeos, after the latest challenge of the announcer. Even Lyaeos looked on him with compassion, saying that he was an athlete, not an executioner. Helianos recognized the young athlete. It was the thin young man who had been sitting next to him and who had run out of the stadium a little while before! Where had he gone, only to come back with such a dangerous decision?

Helianos' indifference gave way to surprise and admiration when he saw the young man taking up the sword and holding it adroitly towards the giant, who was ready to attack him.

"The God of Demetrios, help me!" Everyone in the amphitheater heard his voice as clear as crystal and saw his hand move like lightning.

The swift stroke was made! Lyaeos swayed, bent and collapsed immobilized on the thin sand, while frightful screams like the noise of an earthquake burst out from the chests of all the spectators.

"Oohhhh!" they shouted.

"Lyaeos has been defeated!"

"Who is Demetrios?" Helianos asked the people in the row in front of him, fearfully.

"The Consul …," someone answered.

"A Christian who is in prison!"

"Death! They all deserve death!"

"Death? Why?" Helianos could not contain his surprise.

"Death!"

"But he won! Do they ever kill the winners?" Helianos protested.

"Do you know what it's like for us to lose a great warrior like Lyaeos because of a *Christian?* He should be punished! All of them should be punished! Not even one of them should be left alive on the face of this earth!" yelled someone near him.

Their veins protruded on their temples and throats as they screamed again with hateful voices, "Death!"

"Death!" the word echoed from one section, then from another, and then from the whole amphitheater.

It was true that the Emperor was the judge, but in judging he also had to consider the desire of the people. What was so important about the laws of the stadium and the games that the winner should be rewarded and cheered? Because the winner was a Christian, they could break the rules without any shame. Who would ask them if they were right, anyway?

Diocletian dispensed with every hesitation and, with an imperial grandeur, gave the order that went from the courtiers to the magganarius[1] who supervised the games, and from him to the executioner:

"Let the winner be beheaded!"

Helianos felt his breath become hot and difficult to draw in.

Did they dare to go so far? Instead of a wreath, instead of the victor's triumph ...

His whole body shivered.

He saw the young winner looking up at the sky with a sweet peace. Then the young man brought his right hand up to his forehead, down to his chest and then from one shoul-

---

1. The *magginarius* was the "Master of Ceremonies," who had control over ancient Greco-Roman arena games.—ED.

der to the other. He then bent his neck peacefully, as if waiting for this end to his victory. His great work had finished.

The power of his God had appeared.... Nothing else was important to him. Along with him, Helianos bent his head. No, he didn't want to see. He did not want to see the unexpected outcome of this surprising victory. He felt a deep disgust for the inhuman ferocity that had built its throne in their society, and he whispered inside himself with watery eyes, *"You may be put to death, heroes! You may be killed, Christians! Death is taking away your life, but it doesn't take away your victories and your glory. With your passing, you are leaving us with something great that cannot be erased!"*

Then he remembered the young martyrs in Egypt, and especially the youngest of all, who had given him his last look before he placed his head on the burning charcoals. So the Christians were the same everywhere!

The heavy footsteps of six soldiers who were marching out implied that another new order was to be executed. The guilty one, the great guilty one, was someone else. He was imprisoned nearby, near the public baths. He was the teacher. He was the fiery inspiration. He had to be punished immediately.

The news spread quickly around the stadium. The lances of the soldiers had killed him instantly. Demetrios, the young functionary, the "Consul of Hellas," who had attracted so many of his fellow countrymen to the Lord's faith—some even said that a single day would not go by without him converting another idolater to Christ!—was no longer alive. Galerius and Diocletian and their friends could live in peace now!

As Helianos was waiting outside of the stadium for General Teaos, he saw in the darkness of a nearby alley four men respectfully holding a body wrapped in a sheet. *They are probably going to bury the martyr,* he thought. What honored soil it was that would hold him! What an honored city was Thessalonica, where this great saint was revealed!

The next day Helianos was free from his duties and he went to visit the house of his uncle, his father's brother whom he had never met. The few letters they in Nicomedia had received from Thessalonica had informed them about their relatives' health, their properties and their fruit plantations outside of the city, which with their many rivers and springs always gave them rich harvests. But these letters were never able to keep the ties very close between the two families. Helianos only knew the names of his relatives and remembered his grandfather's praises of his cousin.

He walked on the hilly road that reached the highest point of the city, at the base of Mount Kissos, and came to the house with the arched alleyway, as he had been directed to go. The stillness that prevailed in the garden and the yards implied that the owners were somewhere else, since they were not out enjoying this sweet autumn day that was bathing the whole of nature in sunlight.

But he did find his aunt there. Full of emotion, she welcomed him in the large hall. Although she was petite, she seemed to him especially imposing in her dark robe. Her look was thoughtful and she gazed straight into his eyes as if she was searching for something.

She then had him sit on a bench with carved peacocks on the sides, and asked him with special interest about his family. Since she did not know about his mother's imprisonment, Helianos decided not to mention it. For his part he asked about everyone. But as the conversation continued, Helianos was surprised not to hear a word about his older cousin. The noble lady sighed and then remained silent.

"And Nestor? How is Nestor doing?" he asked, anxious and impatient.

Tears began falling on her cheeks and made him uneasy. Why wasn't she talking? Had something happened to his unknown but beloved cousin whom he was so eager to meet, since he was the only one close to him in age and they would have so many things to talk about concerning the future?

"Nestor!" she whispered with lips trembling.

"Tell me, Aunt! Did something happen?"

He felt close to her, hurting inside in sympathy for her unknown pain.

"Is he ill?" he asked.

"Didn't you hear, yesterday … about the stadium?"

"I heard! And I saw … I was there!"

"Nestor was there …"

"And?"

"He … it was he … who was beheaded!"

Helianos jumped up.

"The one who defeated Lyaeos? *The Christian?*"

"Yes."

"Oh!" he gasped, wringing his hands together in desperation.

Irrepressible tears flowed from his eyes and his lips began to tremble. The shock that had shaken his soul in the arena now became greater, overwhelming and agonizing.

"I did not only see him as a winner. I saw him as the

bravest hero because of what he decided," he whispered with awe.

"He always had a fearless and strong will. But after he became a Christian he became even more daring. He was living the strength of his faith so deeply that he was not afraid of anything."

"Before his announcement that he would fight the giant, he ran somewhere outside of the stadium," Helianos recalled.

"He went to his teacher's prison. I learned that Demetrios prayed with him and told him that he would defeat Lyaeos, and that he would then become a martyr for his faith."

"He told him that?"

"Yes! But that did not dissuade him," his aunt said dejectedly.

"When I saw him yesterday as a martyr, I said to myself, 'You may be killed, Christians, but you are leaving us something great that nobody can erase!' Now, instead I would say, 'You may be killed, Christians, but others will take your place and accept your faith because of you!' "

And Helianos eyes sparkled! But this time they sparkled differently.

13

"NOMINE CHRISTIANORUM DELETO"

H E opened the golden box, which was adorned with rhomboid shapes of red enamel, and, with difficulty, his hardened face broke into a smile. The rays of spring's evening light went through the marble parapet of the balcony with its blossoming roses, passed the ivory recliner with the gold-embroidered arm coverings, reached the alabaster of the side table and, washing over the golden box, illuminated the brand-new gold coins. The long, narrow, finely engraved letters that dominated the face of the coins gleamed in the sunlight.

"At last!" the Emperor said, taking one of the coins in his palm.

He turned it to one side and then to the other, and his weird, difficult smile installed itself on his lips, expressionless and immobile, as he read the long and narrow embossed letters again and again. The weird smile stayed there for a while.

"At last!" he whispered again, and let his gaze go around the city below.

His victory was complete. No longer could the huge cathedral of the Christians be seen. None of their churches remained standing. George no longer existed in the Imperial

Guard. Neither did Hindis, the Senator, or the rest of his courtiers. No longer did the palace priestess, Domna,* exist. Nor did ... he grimaced at the indiscreet thought that had dared to upset his peace. He coughed hoarsely and held the new coins tighter in the palm of his hand and continued his thoughts.

—*So, there was no Empress Alexandra either!*

There was no more Pelagia,* his son's fiancée, whom her own mother had turned in when she became a Christian. She had indeed deserved the copper furnace in the shape of a bull, in which he had her killed! Neither was there the well-known Evilasios.* He had personally sent him on a mission to convert a rich Christian maiden, Fausta,* in the city of Kyzikos, but instead he had become a Christian himself, along with the Eparch Maximus!* Gone were the philosopher Menas,* and the Eparch Hermogenes,* who had become a bishop of the Christians after having first been a persecutor of them. There no longer remained a whole host of military officers and administrative functionaries, so numerous that he could not remember them all. And of course, a plentiful portion of the general population were no more.

There was no doubt that his mind was brilliant! Was he not, after all, the great brain of the whole Empire? That other co-Emperor, Maximian, Augustus of Rome, was only carrying out the inspiration that he, Diocletian, had created. And he was right this time, too.

But he wanted to hear it from someone else's mouth. He wanted to hear it said that, in the past two years, his decrees had succeeded in making him the sovereign master of the very souls of the people.

"Get your parchments, Eumenios, and draw near!"

The hand that was writing with the white quill pen on the other side of the balcony stopped. He placed the finely shaped tip of the pen in the ink bottle and took down the leather case with the wrapped parchments. As the secretary of the Emperor, Eumenios inscribed onto expensive parchments the laws and the letters that Diocletian dictated to him, which the carriages of the Imperial Postal Service sent all around the country, covering more than a hundred miles per day. Moreover, he had also begun writing the biography of his great master, and he kept a note of every incident that would help to enrich his work. That work would give everlasting glory to both of them.[1]

His steps echoed steadily on the mosaic floor with its colorful scenes. But before he even came close to the Emperor's seat, Diocletian's voice stopped him.

"Tell me: are they gone? What do your notes say? You put it on parchment and I put it on gold, but didn't we write the same thing?"

He grabbed one of the coins and threw it towards him. Eumenios picked it up from the floor and read the inscription. All he had to do was to praise his master's new idea with infinite flattery, as always.

"O divine August One! The gods speak to you constantly through your thoughts and works! Your orders are being carried out by all the Consuls, the Eparchs and the Praetors[2] of your kingdom with absolute faith in you, and with the ut-

---

1. This biography of the Emperor Diocletian has been lost.—AUTH.

2. *Praetors* were imperial officials, ranking below Consuls and Eparchs, who acted as provincial magistrates and chief administrators.—ED.

most precision. They are trying their best to erase the name of the Christians from the face of the earth! And they will do it! For you, divine August One!"

He took the thickest parchment out of its case and added, "Here I gather the trophies! And they are your trophies, Emperor: all the names of the disloyal ones who are no longer polluting this earth. In the new victory that you will achieve one day soon, you won't have the images of vanquished kings behind your chariot, but rather that of all those who were correctly punished by your right judgment."

"Are there many of them, Eumenios?"

"Oh! They are infinite, August One!"

"Go ahead! Read! I'm listening! Read!"

The secretary unwrapped the parchment and started counting the names of the Christians who had been executed over the last two years, skipping the ones that Diocletian remembered.

"Those who were punished with a cruel death, my king, are: Count Eudoxios* in Melitini. Member of Parliament Loukios* from Kirini. The ex-Eparch of Alexandria, Prokopios,* along with his two Tribunes, Antiochos* and Nikostratos,* his mother Theodosia* and twelve* functionaries, wives of the Senators who were present at his execution and also rejected the faith of our gods. Also, Sebastian* in Rome, who was the head of the first regiment of the Praetorians, as well as four wealthy Senators, Vassos, Eutechios, Eusebios and Vasilides.* The daughter of Senator Philophron, Euphemia,* in Chalcedon. The lady Capitolina* in Cappadocia.

"You still haven't told me anything interesting!" the Emperor cut him off, frowning. "Go on, continue!"

"There are also the leaders of the Christians that we eliminated, your majesty! In addition to the Bishop of Nicomedia and the priests, Hermolaos,* Hermippos* and Hermokrates,* there were Bishop Theopemptos* and Bishop Philonidis* in Cyprus. Cyril* in Crete, and Theodore* in Kyrini. Bishop Nicholas[1] of Myra is exiled and in prison. I also found out that a reputably wise young lady from Alexandria, Catherine,* the daughter of the sovereign Constas, has been imprisoned...."

"We are not doing anything with such small numbers, you idiot! Don't you get it?"

"But these are not only the ones we've counted, divine August One! I've got big numbers here!"

Eumenios rolled out the parchment and started pointing out the names that he was reading. This time he was certain that he would please the Emperor.

"My most-respected Greatness, you would probably remember that soldier named Hahze."*

"Yes!"

"Along with him, one hundred and fifty soldiers were beheaded when they were sent to arrest him and became Christians under his influence. Your Majesty probably also remembers that brother and sister, Eulambios* and Eulambia,* who were executed. Along with them two hundred* spectators were killed when they followed their belief. You would also remember Juliana,* that rich noble girl who was

---

1. Saint Nicholas, Bishop of Myra, one of the best known and loved of Orthodox saints, was renowned in real life for his great deeds of charity and frequent almsgiving, and became the inspiration of the modern legend of "Saint Nick" or "Santa Claus." He is also patron saint of travelers and seafarers.—Ed.

going to marry Eleusios, the Senator and Eparch of Nicomedia, and had the nerve to ask for him to be baptized as a Christian first! One hundred and thirty women and five hundred men were killed at the same time with her."

"More! Read more!" moaned Diocletian, like a beast excited by the smell of blood.

He moved on his seat irritably, wrinkling the gold-embroidered arm covers, and looked at the parchment with fiery eyes.

"Then there are one thousand one hundred and eighty-four soldiers that Count Eudoxios* converted to Christianity...."

"What happened to that crowd of a thousand who had the nerve to demonstrate in Nicomedia, asking for the persecutions to be ended? Did you try to convince them otherwise?"

"None of them were convinced. We executed them all, my king! There were one thousand and three! And a couple of days ago I heard the news about Andrew,* the officer. General ..."

"So, what about him?" the Emperor interrupted.

"He and his soldiers managed to defeat the Persians in a very difficult campaign. But afterward, they said that the soldiers had come to believe in Christ under his influence, and the Arch-general disbanded the army corps and wanted to send them all home with a guard of a thousand men."

"Are you going to tell me now that they all lapsed morally?"

"Precisely, O wise August One! Two thousand five hundred and ninety-three men, to be exact, were killed at once so that the army would be disciplined! Then we have twenty thousand people* who were inside the church that was burned here in Nicomedia; another three thousand six hundred and eighteen* who were arrested from the hills around the city and were executed; another twenty thousand who were executed in Hermoupolis of Illyria; and more ...”

"Read here! Read so you see what our new coin says! Read the triumph that will be announced around the world, around the whole universe! Read about my triumph, which so many nations are going to learn about, and which history will record for the generations of people to come!”

"*'Nomine Christianorum deleto!'*" read the secretary. "*'To the annihilated name of the Christians!'* Many years, divine Caesar!”

"It will bear witness and remind the whole world that they existed once upon a time, but that every trace of them was erased along with their name, except on my coin!”

Diocletian threw a handful of coins from the golden box to the tireless flatterer and stood up with a wild joy.

"*Nomine Christianorum deleto!*" he shouted, as an ugly laughter erupted from his red face.

"*Nomine Christianorum deleto!* Ha, Ha! *To the annihilated name of the Christians!* Your great victory has been fulfilled, O gods! The Christians do not exist anymore! Their God has been blotted out! Their name has vanished! In a few years no one will even remember that they existed!”

His thunderous voice echoed outside on the large balcony of the palace, went through the marble parapet with the blossoming roses, and reached the garden with the roebucks, the peacocks and the exotic plants.

With its huge tail fanned open, the white peacock was proud of its unusual beauty. Compared with the other two peacocks, whose blue, green and gold feathers and velvety, shiny tails were embellished with big green and blue elongated dots, its colors seemed more brilliant and beautiful on the gleaming golden-white plumage. This bird, brought by the Emperor's experienced hunters who would travel all the way to the far-off forests of India for the skins of wild animals, was the most beautiful decoration of the garden. This fact was evident as the bird walked slowly between the bushes with its tall crest held high on its elegant head and its panoramic tail outstretched.

Suddenly it ran off squawking and hid frightened in the trees. The sound of fast-paced running was heard, lightly, ethereally across the freshly watered lawn. Then a pair of feet jumped agilely over the artificial grotto that gave its shade to the pool of goldfish, and as the last rays of the sun shone, the feet stood on their toes. A young body stretched and a voice as loud and as clear as a trumpet was heard saying, "No, Emperor! No! Christ lives! Christians live! And they will live forever!"

The voice stopped to take a breath.

"The Christians live! One is arrested and a hundred become believers! Ten die and a thousand take their place! Remember, Emperor, the martyrs you knew in person, and you will understand the miracle that supports their faith. Its strength is the Truth, and the Truth never dies! It never vanishes, Emperor!"

The time had come. He said everything with one beat of his heart, with only one breath. His desire was deep and his youthful ambition was to talk to Diocletian, to touch his heart, to convince him about his sacred faith, his almighty faith. And so he found that the time to manifest it could no longer wait...

The August One was enraged. With a livid face, he bent over the marble parapet of the balcony like a wild beast that smelled its prey.

"Who said that? Death to the spy! Soldiers! Guards! Where are you, cowards?"

In the shade of the trees and the dimming light of the sunset, he could not distinguish where the voice had come from. It was quiet for a while, and then the crystal voice was heard again.

" 'Gird Thy sword upon Thy thigh, O Mighty One, in Thy comeliness and in Thy beauty.' 'Thine arrows are sharp, O Mighty One, under Thee shall peoples fall!' Our Christ, August One, is the only Mighty One, no matter how many empires will fight against Him throughout the ages!"

Suddenly two strong hands grabbed the young man by the shoulders and yanked him back.

"Save yourself, brother! Through this door! They're coming! Don't put your life in danger for no reason," a voice cried out.

Mertios, the Christian servant of the imperial palace, who had supported the Church and the faithful on many occasions during these difficult times, appeared at that moment with his quick mind and his warm heart as a guardian angel. He thought that, although the young man had not been afraid to make his brave confession right under the shadow of the Emperor, he certainly did not have to fall into their hands for no reason.

He pushed the young man hard into a small, low opening that was hidden between the bushes and led out into a small, quiet street, and then he closed the opening, camouflaged with a double layer of rock, behind him. It was through this opening in the garden that he and the rest of the Christian brothers and sisters of the palace would go at night to meet their fellow Christians. Then, as he saw the young man disappearing in the dark, tall and well built with his military uniform and his lively walk, Mertios' eyes flashed in recognition. Yes! He remembered!

"Isn't that Helianos, the son of Urvinos the fabric trader? One more conquest of our Lord!" he said to himself. His heart leapt inside. "What a great age of witnesses! How deep and untold are Your joys! How festive You must be with Your brave martyrs, O Lord!"

Tears of joy ran down from his eyes, as he lifted up the box of lemons that he had just picked and disappeared into the trees. A few minutes later, when the soldiers searched the whole garden inch by inch, they did not find anyone or anything suspicious. Could the Emperor possibly have been mistaken?

14

FACING THE GREAT HOUR

H E knocked at the gate for the second time, but no one showed up. There was not an open window in the house, and he could not see a light through the cracks. Helianos looked around, not knowing what he should do.

A few hours before, he had arrived in Nicomedia with the royal postal carriage bringing some epistles and documents from General Teaos to the Emperor. Once he had delivered them to the Chief of the Guard, he had waited to see whether or not there would be an answer to any of the mail. When they had informed him that he did not have to stay, and he had been about to leave, the African guard who had been standing by the door of the garden, knowing that Helianos was the General's new protégé who had just come back from the land of the Nile, had started asking him questions about his native country.

Since his shift was ending, he had the chance to talk to the new arrival and had asked him to wait in the garden. An urgent order from the guard's officer had sent him off on another assignment, leaving Helianos waiting among the exotic plants and the peacocks, without anyone knowing of his presence there. It was then that he had heard Diocletian's triumphant voice celebrating the extermination of the Christians.

Here is my chance! he had thought, and his heart had beat faster.

His old ambition to serve the Emperor someday had become, after what he had witnessed during the past two years, a flaming desire to stand in front of him and confess his new faith that was being persecuted so much. It was *his* faith now!

The big change had happened in Thessalonica, that beautiful city on the Thermaikos Gulf. There the decision had matured. Why shouldn't he become a Nestor or a Demetrios? Weren't they the same as he? Didn't they have the same heart? The same mind? It was worth it to desire such a victory as theirs while he was still young! Not a triumph that would remain on the marble stones of an arch somewhere! Not a triumph that would consist of a tall chariot drawn by gold-adorned elephants, dragging behind it defeated sovereigns as spoils of war and accompanied by drums and trumpets and music, like the one he had seen in Rome a year and a half before in honor of the two co-sovereign August Ones!

They had spent so much money. They had offered huge amounts to all the provinces of their Empire. They had generously offered amnesty to all the convicts, the prisoners and the criminals. Only the Christians had been excluded from this amnesty! Was it because the tyrants recognized that the Christians' triumph was superior to the majesty of the imperial procession with its gilded elephants, banners and conquests? Yet it was this triumph, the silent and serene triumph of the Christians, hidden from the eyes but so amazing in the depths of the heart, that Helianos had desired.

He had found a priest in an out-of-the-way quarter of Thessalonica, and full of inspiration he had found the

Christian truth, the religion of his mother. The desire burned strongly inside him. Should he write to her about the great event? But how could he announce it? By sending a letter to his family? They would not send such news to her. Of course, Pavla was still writing to him with much love for their mother, who was still in prison. But he wasn't sure if this love and tenderness would remain the same if she found out about his conversion. Perhaps this information would be enough to push his father and her into another accusation against his imprisoned mother, with dire consequences.

Should he write directly to his mother? But, as had happened with the first one he had tried to send her, she would never receive his letter! He didn't know any Christians in Nicomedia besides Natalia, but she too, he had learned, did not live there anymore.

Then some Christian travelers had offered to convey a symbolic message to the Church of Nicomedia for him. But sadly, just before entering the city, they had been arrested. And so his intense desire had remained unfulfilled, and his longing was to return to his country as soon as possible. Teaos probably read his mind and gave him just the chance he needed by sending him with the royal mail delivery.

Without feeling tired from the long journey, without being afraid of the anger of his father and his siblings, Helianos had arrived in Nicomedia along with the first sunset rays of the evening, shining with joy. His Christian mother's prison seemed shinier than their beautiful house, and incomparably more elegant than the palace. Innumerable times during his journey he had imagined the time when he would meet her again. He would run to her cell and cry out, "My dear

Mother! I told you once that I'd never become a Christian! But now I'm telling you that I will remain a Christian forever!" With this phrase he would let her know!

So he would go straight to the prison after he had delivered the mail. Why should he keep her away from this joy, even if it was just for one night? But now, after the incident at the royal garden and without knowing what had happened with the African guard, he was sure that the Emperor's people would be looking for him, first at his house and then at the prison. It wasn't wise then to remain in danger, as he had heard from the elders that he should be careful.

The first name that came to his mind was that of his old teacher, Lactantius. He was the Empire's most famous teacher of rhetoric, and had been invited to Nicomedia to help promote the development of education in this new capital. But there were not many in this clearly Hellenic city who were interested in Latin language studies, and Lactantius was engaged much of the time in writing philosophical treatises. Helianos had attended some classes with him and believed that he would readily accept him for one night now, since his house was outside of the city walls and the night was as dark as pitch.

He knocked on the door several times but no one answered. From afar he heard the galloping of a rider who seemed to stop in the yard next door, and he thought that he could probably give him some information. Helianos walked towards him.

"Do you know if the teacher is away?" he asked quietly.

In the darkness, he saw the unknown rider drop his saddlebag abruptly and, turning to him surprised, say, "Helianos, is that you?"

Helianos was startled for a moment. He thought his ears were deceiving him.

"Who is it?... Rhodon? Rhodon is that you? Are you alive?!"

He thought he must be dreaming. Pavla had written to him that the whole Academy of Babylas had been killed, including his old friend Rhodon. How could he be hearing his voice now? He could never forget his friend's voice, but what was that on his face?

Seeing his hesitation, Helianos continued warmly with tears in his eyes, "Don't be afraid of me, Rhodon! I am a Christian now, too!"

"Oh, bless you! I have prayed so much for that!" he exclaimed, hugging his old friend and kissing him on the forehead with brotherly love.

As Helianos embraced him, he felt a deep wound on the side of his friend's neck and pulled himself away with a feeling of awe. Had he just touched a martyr?

"Tell me what happened," he whispered, and stood in front of him with respect.

Yes, Rhodon was alive, even if he had faced death fearlessly and steadily.

"I wasn't worthy of the glorious martyr's wreath," he said humbly, "and the Lord let me prepare. I was last in the line of the eighty-four* students of our school, and I guess the executioner was tired from his dreadful work and didn't hit me with a lot of strength. The Christians who came to pick up our bodies realized that I was still alive. They secretly brought me to this house instead of to my own home and they took care of me for many months, until my open wound was completely healed. The rest are glorified martyrs in heaven. But the Lord left me here to prepare myself...."

"So you can work for His Glory!" Helianos encouraged him.

"Whatever we can do for the faith, we should do it," Rhodon continued. "Every Christian believer needs to hear that inner voice that says, 'Woe to me if I don't spread the good news!' And we should all feel tonight's event: another fifty of our fellow citizens will start their catechism lessons, and guess who is among them?"

"Who?"

"The executioner who struck me! Great are the accomplishments of our faith!"

"What a great and amazing thing, and at the same time so joyful!"

Helianos took a deep breath and then asked impetuously, "How is my mother, Rhodon?"

"Your mother? Didn't you know that they freed her?"

"They set her free? Is she at our home? I didn't know anything. I haven't been home yet. Tell me what happened! Oh, my Lord! Thank you!"

"An officer at the prison made the excuse that there was no room in the cells for the real criminals, in order to free some harmless old men and women, and he managed to secure their release. Nothing can stop me from thinking that a ray of grace shone inside him!"

"And my father? My brother and my sisters? How did they welcome her?"

"Your father is still on a business trip these days, so he is not aware of it yet. As for your brother and sisters, I don't imagine that your little Ione objected to it at all!"

"Ione? No, I mean Pavla and Antiochos!"

"Listen, my dear brother Helianos. Why should I spoil the greatest events in your house with my clumsiness? Go as fast as you can to enjoy the happiness of your home. You asked me a little while ago about the teacher. Learn now that Lactantius was a Christian and he resigned instantly from the position to which the Emperor had appointed him. No one knows where he is now. It is not inconceivable that he is in a prison somewhere. Do you need me to help you with something else?"

"No," he said joyfully, "I don't need anything else anymore!"

Helianos briefed him as to why he was at the teacher's house, and as it was already daybreak on Sunday they bade each other farewell until later that day, when they would meet again—this time at a secret church in the country. Leaving his friend, he began running through the streets of Nicomedia. No fear of the Emperor's search for him could be an obstacle to the ocean of joy that was overwhelming him inside. He ran without feeling tired, seemingly without touching the ground. With the yearning he felt, nothing had the power to stop him or to slow him down, now that he would at last be in his Christian home!

But suddenly, around a corner, a crowd of people holding lighted torches and talking with loud voices and gestures, made him stop.

"Hey you, soldier! Are you running to catch that young Christian, too? He ran away from us!" a short man with a wild face yelled at him.

"Where did he go?" Helianos asked with interest.

The duty and need to help the young Christian who was in danger of falling into their hands arose inside him more strongly than the longing to go home. He had to protect him by all means.

"If you're fast, turn and go straight to the market. Two or three guys have left to get him already, but it seems to me that you will get there faster. That little viper was hiding something!"

"Just when you think that all of them are gone, you meet them again from all sides of the city! Run, soldier, and get him! Hurrah for your youthful strength!"

There, close to the market place, a thin boy was struggling against two men who were beating him up. Helianos jumped between them with all his might, like the times he used to when he was training at the gym. He pushed one man to the left and grabbed the hands of the other with great strength.

"Leave him! I will take care of him!" he said, making his voice sound rough.

The boy turned and looked at him with horror. If it had been daylight, Helianos would have been able to see the waxen paleness on his face. It was Antiochos!

"Oh my Christ! Please do not allow this to happen!" the younger brother could only whisper with pain, his eyes filling with tears.

He was not afraid for himself. He was only anguished that his own brother's heavy hands would fall on him. He felt pain for the torment that their mother would experience. Is that why Helianos had arrived there so suddenly and secretly? So that he could turn in his own relatives to the executioners? Oh, what unbearable guilt for his soul!

What should he do? Should he try to run away? Should he fight with him? Should he ask for mercy for their mother's sake? Like lightning, all these thoughts went through Antiochos' mind in seconds. He knew his brother so well, but one thought stayed with him:

"As much as you may persecute our faith, Helianos, learn that our Christ is undefeated!" he shouted with one breath. "Beat me, if that's what you want, beat me! But you will never be able to beat my Christ, Helianos!"

It was an awful moment for Helianos. A sob welled up in his throat. Every moment that went by in silence, every other word that his brother pronounced, seemed to him like a blasphemy. He abruptly dropped the two men that he had been holding until that moment, and exclaimed with a loud, fearless protest, "Me, beat Christ, Antiochos? His Blood is still running in my veins from the last time I received Holy Communion, a few days ago! I am a Christian, Antiochos!"

The torches that suddenly appeared around the corner made Helianos guess the outcome.

"And I always will be!" he added, signaling with his hand for Antiochos to leave.

There was no time left for anything else. A powerful slap to his face obscured his last words and made his lips bleed.

"A soldier! A traitor! A soldier who is an enemy of our nation!" an angry voice was heard saying, only to be joined by another, and then another and finally many others.

The crowd with the torches attacked him in a frenzy. His tall athletic figure seemed even loftier in the dim light. With every move his lance and sword rattled in their sheaths. But now Helianos was not the strong son of Urvinos, the pride of his gym instructor and of his general, the exceptional candidate for the Imperial Guard who could show his power and skill with his weapons. Now Helianos was a Christian! A Christian in the hands of his persecutors. A Christian who had confessed his faith!

The young soul stood there brave, undefeated.... And then his legs bent, and his body, covered with blood from the many lance strokes he had received, lay motionless on the slates of the street....

"Oh, no! He is the Emperor's favorite!" somebody yelled with fear. "We are doomed!"

"The Emperor's favorite?"

Upon hearing the news, the brave defenders of the idols were shocked and scattered instantly. Blowing out their torches, they disappeared and ran into the darkness.

15

THE PURPLE MANTLE

A soft hand caressed his forehead and smoothed back his hair. Some drops fell from above onto his cheeks and eyelids, and refreshed his burning face. He opened his eyes for a second with difficulty and closed them again slowly. A sweet smile was spread across his face. The soft hand stroked his wounded forehead again and then tenderly lifted up his head.

"My Helianos! My child!" he heard a soft, trembling whisper.

The well known, beloved voice that he had thought about with so much nostalgia over the past two years could not give him back the lost strength to talk and to say everything the way he had planned to. He only had enough power to maintain the smile, spread it across his face, and to show with it a small ray of the sun of his joy.

The bright light from the torch that came closer to him made him more alert. He opened his eyes and saw his mother's face. Then, looking at his robe covered with blood, he concentrated all his strength and spoke with a shining face.

"The Purple Mantle, Mother! The Purple Mantle, the most precious ... the most beautiful ... the most brilliant robe.... I wore it!"

The Christian brethren, who along with Tatiani had learned the news from Antiochos and had run to help him, thought that he was delirious. But his mother understood. And her tears, drops of heavenly refreshment, tears of pain and joy mingled together, fell on his forehead, his cheeks and his neck.

"I wore it ... given by Christ ... and for Christ," he gasped. "Thank you ... for your prayers, Mother!"

He closed his eyes and let his head fall down heavily in her hands.

Two strong men lifted the wounded Helianos up from the slates of the street and carried him away with fast strides. The house that had welcomed and cared for Rhodon was again considered the most suitable and secure for this case. The Christian doctor could carry out his job effectively there. Like a father, he would take care of the brave, heroic new brother, who had not hesitated to confess his faith, and who had preferred to put himself in danger in order to save his sickly younger brother, who would not have been able to run away otherwise. Besides, there he would also be far away from the anger of his father, Urvinos, who was expected to return from his business trip at any time. And, if he lived, the clean air of the country would certainly help him heal faster....

Golden, happy rays of light played across the wildflowers and the leaves on this fine spring morning. The rays also played off of their dark blond hair and the sparkle in their eyes, as they walked through the tender young grass. Tall figures ... strong strides.... The color of health bloomed in their young faces along with the spring of joy, while grace and freedom from cares accompanied their conversation.

It was Helianos and Rhodon.

Here in the secluded, picturesque beauty of the countryside they felt free of Diocletian's threats. Here they were in the Kingdom of their Creator, enjoying its serenity and its beauty. They talked passionately about the trophies that had been won during their age of martyrs. Then, as they found themselves up on a little hill that revealed the entire great plain in front of the city of Nicomedia, they stopped suddenly.

"What's happening down there?"

Army lances and helmets were glistening in the sunlight. In the distance they could make out an official array of functionaries and legionaries. Gold and purple colors glittered in the middle of the city, where there was a column with a statue of Zeus. Helianos put his hand above his eyes to shield them from the glare, and whispered in astonishment, "Wow! Unbelievable! The Emperor's throne is there! On the highest pedestal!"

"The Emperor's?" Rhodon wondered. "Can you see clearly?"

"There's no doubt about it!"

No, there was no doubt. He did see the imperial throne. Once upon a time he had observed it insatiably, and had imprinted its every detail deep inside his memory—the high golden back with the fine carvings, the two globes with the precious stones at the handles, the gold-embroidered purple pillows. As far off as it might seem, for someone who knew, it was not difficult to recognize. But what did this mysterious display of the tyrannical sovereign mean? What was the reason behind it?

They had no interest in learning about it, no desire at all to join the crowd that started surrounding the center. They continued their walk through the hills and fields of the countryside in the sun's radiant light, full of the decisions they had made about the present and the future.

After a while they heard a muffled sound that made them turn back. It was not a cheer or a war cry. It was like a gasp, both sudden and relieved at the same time. The official parade was dismissed. The crowd was moving. Some people were running towards the city, while others ran towards the countryside.

"What's happening?" Rhodon asked someone who was walking toward them.

"Didn't you hear the big news? It was Diocletian! Diocletian announced that he is resigning as Emperor!"

"He *resigned?*"

"On his own? Without a revolt?"

"Yes, by himself! Without anybody pushing him to do it! And he convinced Maximian to do the same! Now the August One in the East is Galerius, and Constantios is the August One in the West!"

The man then moved away quickly so he could spread the news to others who were waiting for him.

The two friends stood there speechless, immobile, and ecstatic! They looked down at the plain, at the army that was demobilizing, at the throne that was being transferred by carriage—in exchange for another one! They stared at the shocking reality. Along with the spring blossoms on this first day of May came the collapse of the power of the persecutor of the Christians, who had tried everything to destroy them!

Galerius would take over his position, but would he manage to finish what his father-in-law had not been able to?[1]

Diocletian, the divine Augustus, the greatest, the almighty ... Diocletian, with the powerful and triumphant coins that read *"Nomine Christianorum deleto"*... Diocletian, the Emperor with armies of executioners, was voluntarily taking off his Purple Mantle in order to drape across his bent shoulders nothing more than the weight of the innumerable crimes he had committed and the disgust he had for himself. The distinguished accomplishments of the beginning of his reign were completely overshadowed by its dark ending.

"Oh poor, inglorious, man-made Purple Mantles, with your human wreckage!" Helianos shouted with amazement.

He remembered.

His eyes were filled instantly with tears. Were they tears of repentance? Of compassion? Of gratitude? Or were they tears of joy? Whatever the cause, they quickly became tears of only joy.

They faced the great plain, as if overlooking all the great plains of all the countries on earth that were irrigated by the

---

1. After continuing the cruel persecutions, Galerius issued a decree in A.D. 311 in which he not only suspended the persecutions against the Christians for a time but even admitted the Empire's inability to vanquish the religion of Christ that was spreading through every town, country and social class of the Empire. He even went so far in his decree as to command the Christians to pray to their God for the Emperor and for the salvation of each city! Of the immediate family of this horrible persecutor, his wife Valeria (Diocletian's daughter), as well as his daughter, Vassilissa, became Christians. Vassilissa, the wife of King Maxentios, accepted Christ while present at the martyrdom of Saint Catherine in A.D. 305, and she was subsequently killed by the sword.—AUTH.

peaceful, invigorating, purple river of the blood of the martyrs. In his mind, Helianos looked over all the races and peoples of the earth, beyond all the histories and ages, and saw another Purple Mantle stretched out before him. It was Brilliant! Priceless! Glorious! Eternal! Indestructible!

"Only One remains forever!" he whispered with inspiration.

"The One!" echoed Rhodon.

"The Timeless and Almighty!"

"The One, Whose Kingdom will never end!"

"They will learn this someday, Diocletian and all the rest of His enemies!" finished Helianos.

And they stayed there watching for a long while, bathed in the Light.

✛　　✛　　✛

The End.
And Glory Be to God!

APPENDIX I

An Alphabetical List of Selected Martyrs
Mentioned in the Story, the Dates of their
Commemoration by the Orthodox Church,
and Brief Biographies of the Major
Martyred Saints.

Adrian and Natalia, Martyrs. *Commemorated August 2*
(†fourth century). The Holy Martyrs Adrian and Natalia
contested for the Christian faith during the reign of Emperors Diocletian and Maximian. Adrian, who was a pagan, declared himself to be a Christian upon witnessing the bravery
and the faith of the **Twenty-three Martyrs.**[1] He was imprisoned and his hands and feet were broken off with a hammer.
Natalia, his wife, was a Christian and visited him in prison to
encourage him in his torments. When Adrian died from his
wounds, she recovered part of his holy relics and took them
to the town of Argyropolis, near Byzantium (later known as

---

1. According to the original Life, Adrian was a pagan prior to
witnessing the testimony of the Twenty-Three Martyrs, whereas in *The
Purple Mantle* he is portrayed as having been a Christian before that
event. This is the only major discrepancy we have found between the
Orthodox Lives of Saints and the narrative of this novel. Other, minor
discrepancies occur between the traditional year of martyrdom of
various saints and the sequence that is portrayed in the novel.—Ed.

Constantinople, or present-day Istanbul), where she reposed in the Lord.

Alexandra, Empress, Martyr. *April 21.* This Saint was the wife of the Emperor Diocletian. Having witnessed the martyrdom of Saint George, she declared herself a Christian and was thus subjected to tortures. She finally reposed in the Lord in prison in A.D. 303.

Anatolios and Protoleon, Commanders, Martyrs. *April 23.* These soldiers were converted to Christianity by witnessing the martyrdom of Saint George, and were subsequently martyred themselves in A.D. 303.

Andrew Stratelates, Martyr. *August 19.* Syrian by birth, he was an officer in the Roman army during the reign of Emperor Maximian. When attacked by Syria, Andrew and a select group went out to battle. Revealing his hitherto secret Christian faith, he told his soldiers that if they called on the one true God, Christ the Lord, they would be victorious. They prayed to Christ and indeed defeated the enemy. Afterwards he and his 2,593 soldiers were baptized in Tarsus of Cilicia. Being persecuted by imperial might, they withdrew to Armenia, to Mount Tavros, where they were slain sometime at the end of the third century.

Anikitos (Anicetus) and Fotios (Photius), Martyrs. *August 12.* Saint Anikitos confessed his faith when Diocletian began his persecution of the Christians, and said openly that all those who worshipped idols were blind and senseless. He was beaten with rods until his bones were exposed, and as he was tortured further, his nephew Fotios embraced him and confessed his faith in Christ. The two were imprisoned together for three years and then finally thrown into a furnace, where they reposed in the Lord, their bodies remaining uncorrupted by the flames. Saint Anikitos is one of the Holy Unmercenary Saints of the Orthodox Church.

Anthimos, Bishop of Nicomedia, Hieromartyr. *September 3.* Born in Nicomedia, he was brought up from childhood as a Christian. As a bishop he strengthened the Church through his epistles and visits during the bloody persecution of the Emperors Diocletian and Maximian. When soldiers were sent to find him, he went of his own accord to meet them, inviting them to his house. Only after graciously offering them hospitality did he reveal to them that he was indeed the Anthimos for whom they sought. Although urged to hide, he resolutely returned with the soldiers, teaching them the Christian faith and converting them on their way to Nicomedia, where he was tortured and finally beheaded with an axe in the year 302.

Antiochos, Martyr. *See* Prokopios, Great Martyr.

Apollos, Isaakios and Kodratos (Quadratus), Martyrs. *April 21.* These members of the entourage of Empress Alexandra converted to Christianity upon witnessing the martyric testimony of their queen, and were subsequently martyred themselves in A.D. 303.

Babylas of Nicomedia, Martyr, and Eighty-four Children with Him. *September 4* (†A.D. 304).

Capitolina of Caesarea in Cappadocia, Martyr. *October 27* (†A.D. 304).

Catherine of Alexandria, Great Martyr. *November 25.* A young noblewoman of exceptional beauty and education, Catherine refused to marry any suitor whom she deemed to be less than her equal in intelligence. After a Christian Bishop revealed to her that she would find the bridegroom she was seeking only through intensive prayer, she had a vision of Jesus and became a fervent Christian. Through her God-inspired wisdom and her rhetorical skills, she stopped the mouths of the ungodly idolaters. When she refused to deny her faith, the great Saint was subjected to the most inhuman tortures, from which she emerged unscathed. After converting many people to belief in the true God, she was finally beheaded and thus received the crown of martyrdom about A.D. 305.

Constantine Chlorus, Equal-to-the-Apostles and Right-Believing King.[1] May 21 (†A.D. 327). St. Constantine is well known for his victory over Maxentius with the help of the sign of the Cross, and also for the Edict of Milan of A.D. 313, by which he made it permissable to practice the Christian faith. He summoned the First Ecumenical Council in 325, which formulated the Nicean Creed (amplified at the Second Ecumenical Council) and which set a common date for all of Christendom to celebrate Holy Pascha ("Easter"). His reign inaugurated the "Byzantine Era" of Christianity, a golden age of Christian culture which lasted for eleven hundred years.

1. St. Constantine was not a martyr, but is listed here as a Saint who is mentioned in this book.—ED.

Cyril of Crete, Hieromartyr. *September 6 and July 9* (third-fourth century). Bishop of Gortyna in Crete, St. Cyril at the age of eighty-four was tortured and thrown into fire. After being miraculously delivered from the fire, he was beheaded. This happened during the reign of Decius.

Demetrios the Myrrh-gusher of Thessalonica, Great Martyr. *October 26* (†A.D. 306). This Saint, one of the most revered of the Orthodox Church, was from Thessaly in Greece. He was born of a noble family of pious Christians, and at a young age became a fervent teacher of the Christian faith. Demetrios was elevated to the status of Duke of Thessalonica in 290, but when it was discovered that he was a Christian, he was arrested and held in chains in a bathhouse. During games in the stadium, a well known wrestler and gladiator, Lyaeos, challenged the citizens to a contest with him and all were defeated. However, a disciple of the Saint, Nestor, went and received Demetrios' blessing to do battle with the barbarian in single-combat. Nestor cried out to the "God of Demetrios" for help and then defeated the pagan with a single blow, whereupon the Emperor had the Saint run through with spears while he was still chained in the bathhouse. The victorious **Nestor** *(commemorated on October 27)* was commanded to be executed with his own sword.

Dorotheos, Martyr. *See* Twenty Thousand Martyrs.

Domna, Martyr. *See* Twenty Thousand Martyrs.

Eighty-four Students, Martyrs. *See* Babylas, Martyr.

Eudoxios of Melitene, Martyr. *September 6* (†A.D. 311). This Saint was a Christian of noble birth from Melitene, on the border of the Roman Empire with Armenia. He and his friends **Zenon** and **Makarios** were martyred, along with **one thousand one hundred and eighty-four soldiers** of the cohort that had been sent to arrest him and were converted to Christianity through him.

Eulambios and His Sister Eulambia, Martyrs. *October 10* (†A.D. 296). This brother and sister from Nicomedia martyred for the faith along with **two hundred** spectators who confessed Christ and were martyred with them.

Euphemia the All-praised, Great Martyr. *September 16.* This virgin-martyr was born in Chalcedon to an aristocratic family. Despite her wealth and position, she devoted her life to works of Christian charity. During Diocletian's persecutions, she was arrested and brought before the temple priests to worship the idols. When she refused, she was imprisoned, tortured and finally thrown to the wild beasts in the arena, in A.D. 304.

Eusebios of Nicomedia, Martyr. *See* Vassos, Martyr.

Eutechios, Martyr. *See* Vassos, Martyr.

Evilasios, Martyr. *See* Fausta, Virgin Martyr.

Fausta, Virgin Martyr, and with Her Evilasios and Maximos of Kyzikos (Cyzicus), Martyrs. *February 6.* This thirteen-year-old girl was martyred in Cyzicus during the reign of

Maximian (between 305 and 311). Her heroic endurance of tortures converted the eighty-year-old pagan priest Evilasios and the Eparch Maximos, who were themselves subsequently martyred in Cyzicus.

Fotios, Martyr. *See* Anikitos and Fotios, Martyrs.

George the Trophy-bearer, Great Martyr. *April 23.* One of the best-known and loved Saints of the Orthodox Church, George was born of a father from Cappadocia in Asia Minor and a mother from Lydda in Palestine. He was a military tribune, or *chiliarchos* (commander of a thousand), under the Emperor Diocletian, and was highly honored for his valor and success in battle. Upon learning of the persecutions the Emperor was preparing against the Christians, George presented himself before the Emperor and publicly denounced him. When Diocletian could not sway George from his steadfast confession of the Christian faith, he put him through unimaginable tortures. The Saint endured these torments with great bravery through his faith in Christ and love for Him, and he led many, including the Empress Alexandra, to the true faith through his valiant example and the miraculous signs that took place during his martyrdom. The great Saint was finally beheaded in A.D. 303.

Gorgonios, Martyr. *See* Twenty Thousand Martyrs.

Hahze (Azes) of Isauria and One Hundred Fifty Soldiers, Martyrs. *November 19* (†A.D. 284).

Hermogenes, Martyr. *See* Menas, Martyr.

Hermolaos, Hieromartyr, and Martyrs Hermippos and Hermokrates at Nicomedia. *July 26* (†A.D. 305). Saint Hermolaos was a priest in the church of Nicomedia (where the holy twenty thousand martyrs were burned to death), and it was he who converted Saint Panteleimon to Christianity. After being arrested and interrogated as to who had made him believe in Christ, St. Panteleimon had a divine vision that the time for his beloved spiritual father's martyrdom was at hand. He therefore confessed his name to the authorities, who arrested the Saint and his companions. They in turn confessed their faith in Jesus Christ and were beheaded about the same time as Saint Panteleimon.

Hindis, Martyr. *See* Twenty Thousand Martyrs.

Isaakios, Martyr. *See* Apollos, Isaakios and Kodratos, Martyrs.

Hermippos, Martyr. *See* Hermolaos, Hieromartyr.

Hermokrates, Martyr. *See* Hermolaos, Hieromartyr.

Juliana, Martyr. *December 21* (†A.D. 304). Juliana, a secret Christian, was unwillingly betrothed by her wealthy, pagan parents to a member of the senate, Eleusios. Knowing that he was an idolater, the Saint refused the engagement by setting a very difficult condition as her excuse: she told him she would not marry him until he became Eparch (or Duke) of Nicomedia. When he achieved this, she again refused, confessing that she was a Christian and telling him that she would marry him only if he also became one. The Eparch sent her back to her parents to be convinced to deny her faith, but when they failed to change her mind, her father sent her back to Eleusios with his permission to do whatever he wanted to the Saint. He imprisoned her, subjected her to inhuman torments, and finally had her thrown into a giant furnace. When the flames were miraculously quenched and the Saint was delivered unharmed, **one hundred thirty women and five hundred men** who witnessed the event believed in Christ and were beheaded for their faith. Juliana was tortured further and then finally beheaded.

Kodratos, Martyr. *See* Apollos, Isaakios and Kodratos, Martyrs.

Kyriaki, Great Martyr. *July 7.* This great virgin-martyr of the Church was born to devout Christian parents who were themselves arrested and exiled for their Christian activism. When Kyriaki, who was renowned for her great beauty, was about to become a nun, she was arrested by the local authorities because of her confession of faith. Dispelling their attempts to turn her from her faith, she verbally overpowered her captors, and through her prayers a pagan temple was destroyed. The local magistrate intended to have her beheaded, but before this took place she was allowed to pray, and she reposed peacefully on the very spot where she was about to be executed.

Loukios (Lucius), Martyr. *August 20.* A Senator in Cyprus, he was from Kirini and was martyred about A.D. 310.

Maximos, Martyr. *See* Fausta, Virgin Martyr.

Menas, Hermogenes and Eugraphos of Alexandria, Martyrs. *December 10.* Menas and Hermogenes were both born in Athens but lived in Constantinople, where they held high positions in the government. Menas was secretly a Christian, while Hermogenes, although very merciful, was a confirmed pagan. Menas was sent by Emperor Maximian to quell a disturbance in Alexandria. He successfully calmed the people and also openly declared his faith, converting many pagans. Hermogenes was sent to torture and execute Menas, but upon seeing Menas' miraculous healings from the wounds of torture, he too became a believer. The enraged Emperor came himself to oversee their execution, which took place in 313 in Alexandria.

Nestor, Martyr. *See* Demetrios, Great Martyr.

Nikostratos, Martyr. *See* Prokopios, Great Martyr.

Panteleimon [Pantoleon], Great Martyr and Healer. *July 27* (†A.D. 305). Saint Panteleimon was the son of an idolatrous father and a Christian mother. He was a doctor by profession, but he healed more through prayer and his deep faith in Christ than through his skills as a physician. Moreover, he did so without ever charging for his services, and while preaching the gospel of Christ wherever he went. For this reason, although he was named Pantoleon by birth, he became known as Panteleimon, which in Greek means "all merciful." After healing a blind man (who became a Christian and was also martyred for his faith), Panteleimon was arrested, subjected to many tortures and finally beheaded. Saint Panteleimon is held in special honor among the Holy

Unmercenary Saints of the Orthodox Church, and his wondrous miracles of healing are exhibited even to this day to those who call on him in faith.

Paphnutios of Egypt and Five Hundred Forty-six Companions, Martyrs. *September 25* (†third century).

Pelagia, Virgin Martyr. *May 4* (†A.D. 287). Saint Pelagia was from the city of Tarsus of Cilicia, also the birthplace of Saint Paul. When she heard about Christianity and sought to learn more about the faith, she had a dream in which she saw the local Christian Bishop performing baptisms. Pelagia secretly went to the Bishop, who by the inspiration of the Holy Spirit welcomed her warmly and subsequently baptized her. When Pelagia's fiancé, the Emperor's son, heard of her conversion, he was driven to despair and committed suicide. Emperor Diocletian attempted to turn the Saint away from her faith in Christ, but when she refused he had her placed inside a hollow bronze statue of a bull that was heated in an intense fire. Thus the virgin martyr gave herself up for Christ and received the imperishable crown of martyrdom.

Peter, Martyr. *See* Twenty Thousand Martyrs.

Philonidis, Bishop of Curium in Cyprus, Hieromartyr. *June 17.*

Prokopios of Caesarea in Palestine, Great Martyr (former Eparch of Alexandria). *July 8* (†A.D. 303). Prokopios was born of a Christian father and a pagan mother. The Saint's father having died when he was very young, Neanias (as he was called before his conversion to Christianity) was raised as an idolater. Through his mother's influence with the Emperor Diocletian, after completing his education the young man was named Eparch (or Duke) of Alexandria, despite his young age. Soon after his appointment, he was given orders to eliminate the Christian population of that great city. However, as he traveled to Alexandria to carry out his mission, the Saint beheld in the sky a vision of the crucified Lord Jesus Christ, whereupon he and his two military attachés, **Antiochos** and **Nikostratos**, who also saw the Lord, immediately became believers. Instead of persecuting the Christians, they began to preach the gospel of Christ. The Saint was betrayed to the Emperor by his own mother and imprisoned and tortured in Caesarea of Palestine. (It was there, in prison, that he was visited again by the Lord and given the name Prokopios, which comes from the Greek word for "progress" or "advancement.") When the Saint and his fellow Christians were brought before a temple to worship the idols, their prayers caused the idols to fall and the temple to collapse. As a result of this miracle, several more people became believers in Christ, including **twelve women of senatorial rank** and the Saint's own mother, **Theodosia**, and also received martyr's deaths at the hands of the local prefect. Prokopios and his companions were imprisoned once again, tortured, and finally beheaded.

Sebastian of Rome, Martyr, and His Companions. *December 18* (†A.D. 287). Originally from Milan, the Saint was a Roman senator and fervent Christian. Under Diocletian's persecution of the Christians, he and several of his fellow Christians were arrested. The Saint's body was pierced with arrows, his bones were broken with clubs, and he was finally cut into pieces.

Theodore, Bishop of Kyrini (Cyrene) in Libya, Hieromartyr, and with Him Martyrs Kyprilla, Aroa and Lucia. *July 4* (†A.D. 310).

Theodosia, Martyr. *See* Prokopios, Great Martyr.

Theonas, Christopher, Antoninos and Kesarios (Caesarius), Martyrs. *April 20.* These young men were officers under Emperor Diocletian. When they beheld St. George's heroic confession of the faith, they threw down their military belts and proclaimed their allegiance to our Lord Jesus Christ. They were subsequently cast into the fire and burned alive in A.D. 303.

Theopemptos, Bishop of Nicomedia, Hieromartyr, and Martyr Theonas. *January 5.* After St. Theopemptos publicly denounced Diocletian to his face for his ungodliness in persecuting the Christians, he was tortured cruelly, but remained unharmed. He was made to drink poison, but when he remained unharmed, the sorcerer who had prepared the potion was converted to the faith. The Saint was tortured further and finally beheaded, while the converted sorcerer, Theonas, was buried alive. This occurred in A.D. 303.

Three Thousand Six Hundred and Eighteen Martyrs of Nicomedia. *September 2* (third-fourth century).

Twenty Thousand Holy Martyrs Burned in Nicomedia. *December 28.* These Saints, who numbered some 20,000 men, women and children, were all burned alive in A.D. 303, while gathered together in the largest church in Nicomedia. According to the *Synaxaristes of the Saints* of the Orthodox Church, this event took place on the day of Christ's Nativity (Christmas). Also commemorated with these Saints are the holy martyrs **Hindis** (Indes), **Gorgonios** and **Peter**, who were cast into the sea; **Glykerios** the Presbyter and **Mardonios**, who were burned; **Dorotheos** the Prefect and **Zenon**, who were beheaded; **Theophilos** the Deacon, who was stoned; **Mygdonios**, who was burned alive; and **Domna**, a former priestess of the idols, who came to believe in Christ and was baptized, and who was beheaded and then cast into the fire.

Vassos (Bassus), Eutechios (Eutychius), Eusebios and Vasilides (Basilides), Martyrs. *January 20.* They were martyred in Nicomedia in A.D. 303.

Vasilides, Martyr. *See* Vassos, Martyr.

Zenon, Martyr. *See* Twenty Thousand Martyrs.

APPENDIX II

Apolytikion (Troparion) of the Holy Martyrs Adrian and Natalia (TONE 3)

Thou didst deem that faith which hath salvation to be riches never lost or plundered. Thou didst forsake thy fathers' impiety, and thou didst follow thy Master, becoming rich in His divine gifts, O glorious Adrian. With the Godly minded Natalia, who emboldened thee, entreat Christ God, O Martyr, that our souls be saved.

Kontakion of the Holy Great Martyr and Healer Panteleimon (TONE 5)

Since thou art an emulator of the Merciful One, and hast received from Him the grace of healing, O prizewinner and Martyr of Christ our God, by thy prayers heal the diseases of our souls, and ever dispel the stumblingblocks of the enemy from them that cry unceasingly: Save us, O Lord.

Apolytikion of the Holy Glorious Great Martyr George the Trophy-bearer (TONE 4)

Liberator of captives, defender of the poor, physician of

the sick, and champion of kings, O trophy-bearer Great Martyr George, intercede with Christ God that our souls be saved.

Apolytikion of the Holy Twenty Thousand Martyrs Burned in Nicomedia (Tone 2)

Blessed is the earth that drank your blood, O prizewinners of the Lord, and holy are the tabernacles that received your spirits; for in the contest ye triumphed over the enemy, and ye proclaimed Christ with boldness. Beseech Him, we pray, since He is good, to save our souls.

Apolytikion of the Holy Great Martyr Kyriaki (Tone 4)

O Lord Jesus, unto Thee Thy lamb doth cry with a great voice: O my Bridegroom, Thee I love; and seeking Thee, I now contest, and with Thy baptism am crucified and buried. I suffer for Thy sake, that I may reign with Thee; for Thy sake I die, that I may live in Thee: accept me offered out of longing to Thee as a spotless sacrifice. Lord, save our souls through her intercessions, since Thou art great in mercy.

Apolytikion of the Holy Great Martyr Demetrios the Myrrh-gusher (Tone 3)

A great champion hath the world found thee to be when in grave perils; for thou dost put to flight the heathen, O victorious one. As thou didst humble Lyaeos' arrogance and gavest boldness to Nestor in the stadium, thus, O holy Great Martyr Demetrius, do thou entreat Christ God that we be granted great mercy.

Apolytikion of the Holy Great Martyr Catherine (Tone 5)

Let us praise the all-lauded and noble bride of Christ, the Godly Catherine, the guardian of Sinai and its defense, who is also our support and succor and our help; for with the Holy Spirit's sword she hath silenced brilliantly the clever among the godless; and being crowned as a Martyr, she doth now ask great mercy for us all.

Kontakion of the Holy Martyr Juliana (Tone 1)

A comely virgin wast thou, O wise Juliana; and as thy soul was wounded with love for thy Maker, thy body was also pierced through with comely martyric wounds, which adorned thee as the bride of Christ and His Martyr; now as thou dost dwell in the bridechambers of Heaven, thou prayest for all of us.

Apolytikion of Bishop Anthimos (Tone 4)

As a sharer of the ways of the Apostles and a successor to their throne, O inspired of God, thou foundest discipline to be a means of ascent to divine vision. Wherefore, having rightly divided the word of truth, thou didst also contest for the faith even unto blood, O Hieromartyr Anthimos. Intercede with Christ God that our souls be saved.

General Apolytikion for a Martyr (Tone 4)

Thy Martyr, O Lord, in his (her) courageous contest for Thee, received as the prize the crowns of incorruption and life from Thee, our immortal God. For since he (she) possessed Thy strength he (she) cast down the tyrants and wholly destroyed the demons' strengthless presumption. O Christ God, by his (her) prayers, save our souls, since Thou art merciful.

ST. HERMAN OF ALASKA BROTHERHOOD

For over three decades, the St. Herman Brotherhood has been publishing works of traditional spirituality.

Write for our free 96-page catalogue, featuring sixty titles of published and forthcoming books and magazines.

St. Herman of Alaska Brotherhood
10 Beegum Gorge Road
P. O. Box 70
Platina, CA 96076

Typeset in Minion with display lines in Trajan.

*Color separation for cover by Summerfield Graphics,
Santa Rosa, California.*

Printed by Thomson-Shore, Inc., Dexter Michigan.